THE MACMILLAN COMPANY
NEW YORK · BOSTON · CHICAGO · DALLAS
ATLANTA · SAN FRANCISCO

MACMILLAN & CO., Limited
LONDON · BOMBAY · CALCUTTA
MELBOURNE

THE MACMILLAN COMPANY
OF CANADA, Limited
TORONTO

RIDING WEST

ON THE PONY EXPRESS

❦

CHARLES L. SKELTON

ILLUSTRATED BY PAUL QUINN

NEW YORK

THE MACMILLAN COMPANY

1937

AUTHOR'S NOTE

The Pony Express was an exploit as brave, as fine, as any in all the annals of the West. To tell an accurate story of that exploit is not easy. The riders of the Express were boys of action, who hurried on to other adventures as soon as they had stripped the mochilas from the saddles for the last time, without stopping to set down records for writers of a later day.

Riding West has some factual matter never before published, including a correct description of J. A. Slade, the most colorful individual connected with the Pony Express. Alex Carlyle—who rode the Express for a couple of months and died of tuberculosis—his uncle, B. F. Ficklin, Alexander Majors and his partners, and J. A. Slade are historical characters.

I am grateful to many for help in writing this book, and to those who assembled papers and records, answered letters, made suggestions. Special thanks are due Paul M. Angle, librarian, and Anna A. Kosek, assistant librarian, Illinois State Historical Library, Springfield, Ill.; I. R. Bundy, librarian, St. Joseph Public Library, St. Joseph, Mo.; Mrs. Louise Platt Hauck, St. Joseph, Mo.; Mr. Lew L. Callaway, Helena, Mont.; Mr. Burton Carey, Virginia City, Mont.; Mr. Emil Kopac, Oshkosh, Nebr.; Mr. Sewell Peaslee Wright and Miss Orlene Drobisch, Springfield, Ill.

CHARLES L. SKELTON

June, 1937

CONTENTS

RIDING WEST

On the wharf at the foot of Jule Street, Chet and Jeff Harlowe paused. With keen, appraising eyes they looked at the ferryboat, tied up there on the Missouri side of the great river.

Discolored slabs of ice still clung to the river banks, but brown, wind-roughened water ran swift and free out in the main channel, and eddied around the piling of the wharf. High on the bluffs above the landing and straggling down onto the lower ground were the myriad houses and stores of St. Joseph.

The two brothers had never been in so large a town before. It seemed a city to them, this bustling place of nine thousand inhabitants. They had vaguely expected to find here a small trading post, a few stores, perhaps a line of stockaded forts along the river front. For here at St. Joe, as everyone knew, the real West began. Beyond lay the plains, the Indian and buffalo country, the great desert.

"I never knew they had ferryboats as big as that, Chet," said Jeff. "D'you suppose that *is* a ferry? She's as big as a regular river boat!"

"I reckon it's a ferry," the older brother replied. "Here comes a deck hand; we can ask him."

As the colored roustabout strolled closer along the wharf, Jeff spoke: "That's a ferryboat, is it?"

I

"Yas, suh, she shore am, de ferryboat *Denver*." He sent a glance of rolling eyes at the gilt-lettered sign on the boat's pilot house.

"She must take a good-sized load."

"She shore do. A dozen wagons an' teams at a clip, or two hundred haid o' cattle. Dat's on de main deck. An' in de cabin dey's room foh more'n a hundred folks."

The boys stood where they were till the negro had walked on. Then, moved by a single impulse, squaring their shoulders with quick motions, they marched up the broad gangplank. They encountered Captain Blackistone on the main deck, and hastily made their oft-rehearsed inquiry.

"A chance to go West with an outfit!" exclaimed the captain. "Great Scott, boys, how do I know? That's out of my line—my job is to set 'em across the river, and it keeps me busy." He would have turned away, with this, but something in the resolute faces of the lads held him. "If you're in a hurry, the best way to go West is by stage," he added, in a more cordial tone. "There's a stage out of here three times a week for Denver. Makes fast time, only six days to get through."

Jeff involuntarily ran his left hand into his trousers pocket. "How much does it cost to go that way, captain?"

"Seventy-five dollars."

"I don't reckon we'll go that way," Chet said, hastily. "We'll have to figure out something else. Much obliged, sir."

They went down the gangplank, crossed the wharf, and walked up the steep, gravelly road to the upper level of the town. At the top of the hill they turned and looked back

2

across the muddy, hurrying river to the far bluffs on the western side.

Night was coming on under a darkening, stormy sky. The wind blew chill. Jeff pulled his old felt hat down tighter, drew closer to his brother. "I reckon we can get in with an outfit all right, if we keep our eyes peeled. Don't you think so?"

"Don't see why not. You've heard Dad tell many a time how he hooked up with old Cap'n Bent's wagon train."

"Just sort of hung on and wouldn't take no for an answer, didn't he?"

"Yes. And that's the way he come to meet Kit Carson."

"And if he hadn't got in that particular outfit, he'd never've been one of Carson's 'mountain men,' would he?"

"Reckon not."

"Say, Chet, you know that old geography we had when we went to school? Remember that map where it showed the Great American Desert?"

"Yeah, I sort of remember it. Desert was a kind of speckled brown, same as the Sahara Desert. Why?"

"Well, don't that desert begin out here somewheres just a little west of the Missouri River?"

"Supposed to, I reckon. But Dad used to say some years there was mighty good grass all over that country out there."

Chet tucked their small bundle of extra clothing tighter under his arm as he spoke. Jeff tugged at his hat; they walked on up the darkening street. Jeff's left hand, in his trousers pocket, held a little buckskin pouch. His fingers could count the coins through the worn leather, they had done it so often. There still were the two five-dollar goldpieces Grandma

3

Pringle had given him. Besides, he had some silver. Altogether, twelve dollars and seventy-five cents. Chet had money, too—almost twenty dollars.

They paused under the wooden awning of a false-fronted store building Loud voices inside were arguing something strange: "Ten days from here to Californy! Old Majors is crazy! You can't make it in no such time, I tell you!"

They walked on aimlessly, careless of what might be going on around them. Soon they were in the outskirts of the town, past the last yellow radiance of the oil street lights.

A sudden yell startled them. They ran ahead; they came to the dusky corner where a young man, backed against a fence, was battling three others ringed about him.

"What's the matter?" Chet called.

"A holdup! Help!"

The brothers closed in. One of the youths turned savagely on Jeff. Jeff wheeled and ran a few steps with the other on his heels. Then, quick as a flash, he dropped to his hands and knees. His pursuer sprawled over him heavily and lay where he fell.

As Jeff ran back to the struggling group the other two assailants skurried away under a shower of blows from Chet and the man at his side. The chap Jeff had tripped meantime got up and slunk off in the darkness.

"Say, you fellows got here just about the right time," remarked the young man, coolly. He was breathing hard, but seemed unexcited. "I'm mightily obliged to you," he went on. "I might have handled two of them, but three was too many. My name is Alex Carlyle." He held out his hand.

Chet grasped it. "Mine is Chet Harlowe. And this is my brother, Jeff. What were they trying to do, rob you?"

4

"Yes. They found out, or guessed, that I have some money on me. Were you fellows going anywhere in particular?"

"No, just fooling around."

"Had supper?"

"Not yet."

"If you've nothing special to do, come on with me. Know where the Patee House is?"

"Never even heard of it."

"We just got here today—first time we were ever in St. Joe," Jeff added.

"All right, come on. I'll show you something."

They walked back to the yellow street lamps, and on past scattered and then closely set houses. Presently the outline of a large building showed ahead. Lights gleamed from many windows. "That," Alex Carlyle announced, impressively, "is the Patee House."

5

He led the way up the steps and into an imposing lobby. Chet and Jeff had a confused impression of brightly polished brass lamps, of shining columns, and high walls hung with gilt-framed paintings and the antlered heads of deer and elk. They stepped warily across a polished floor and over a large bearskin rug. Through an arched doorway they followed their guide into a great dining room. Tables snowy with napery and gleaming with glass and silver stretched out before them. A dusky-faced, white-clad waiter came up smartly.

"Right this way, genlemum," he greeted.

They followed him to a small table. He slid Jeff's chair under him, and deftly placed bills of fare.

The two brothers gazed blankly at the printed card.

PATEE HOUSE
Supper, Thursday, March 15, 1860

* * * * * *

CONSOMMÉ EN TASSE
TÊTE DE VEAU EN TARTUE

—

FILET DE BŒUF À LA BERNARDI
CÔTELETTES DE PORC FRAIS
HARICOTS VERTS
PETITS POIS
ASPERGE, SAUCE CRÊME
POMME DE TERRE LYONNAISE

—

SOUFFLÉ À L'ORANGE
CAFÉ   THÉ   LAIT
FROMAGE

6

From the card Jeff's gaze roved to the snowy tablecloth, to the array of silverware beside his plate, and on down the long line of tables in the almost deserted room. He was uncomfortably aware of the waiter standing behind him. He saw that his brother was ill at ease. Then the embarrassed tension relaxed at Alex's grin.

Alex addressed the waiter with mock severity: "Jim, I've told you more than once that I don't care anything about these fancy French programs of yours. I'm hungry, and so are my friends. Bring us the best you've got, and plenty of it!"

Alex Carlyle, slender almost to frailness, could not have been more than twenty-two. A smile lit his thin, eager face as he glanced with friendly appraisal at his guests. Brothers indeed they were, he could have seen that for himself without being told. Both were firm-lipped, square-jawed, gray-eyed, alert, their fair-skinned faces showing the color laid by wind and weather. What Alex saw in that keen glance roused his quick liking. His intuitive sensitiveness told him at once that these two were very close to each other.

"You say this is your first visit to St. Joe?" he suggested.

"Yes," Chet answered. "Our folks are dead—we've been living for the last year with some neighbors, but the country back there in eastern Missouri is settled up too much to suit us. We made up our minds to go West. Figured maybe we could get in with some outfit and sort of work our way along. But the way it begins to look, I reckon we'd better find jobs and gather up a stake, first."

Alex gave the boys another reckoning glance, then spoke straightforwardly. "You're game, anyhow. You did me a good turn, maybe I can partly repay it. You've heard of Russell, Majors, and Waddell, I suppose?"

"I saw their names on a sign somewhere here in town today," Jeff said, eagerly.

"Their office is over on Second Street. They're the biggest freighting company in the West. Have the contract for supplying all the Western army posts, and run a stage line from here to Salt Lake City. My uncle, Ben Ficklin, is superintendent of the stage line.

"The officials at Washington are anxious to get better mail service to California. Senator Gwin of California has been talking to my uncle for years about it, and to Mr. Russell. California is away off out there by itself like some separate country—it takes over three weeks for a letter to go from New York or Washington to San Francisco by way of Panama, and pretty nearly that long by the Butterfield stage line. Lately, you know, there's a lot of talk about trouble between the North and the South—I don't think there'll be any war, but the pressure for faster mails to California is increasing. If war should break out, a fast mail line would be mighty important. Anyhow, Russell, Majors, and Waddell have agreed to establish a Pony Express line to carry mail from the Missouri River to California *in ten days*. What do you think of *that?*"

"A Pony Express line?"

"Yes." Alex paused to stifle a cough. A flush of unnatural color was in his cheeks. "They're going to have sixty riders, maybe more," he went on, "young, game fellows they can depend on. They'll get the best horses for 'em that money can buy. When everything is lined up, a rider will

8

start west from St. Joe with the mail in his saddlebags. He'll
hit it up at a good fast clip for about twenty-five miles,
change over to a fresh pony that'll be ready for him at a
station, and ride on, changing and riding till he's made
seventy-five miles. Then a fresh rider with a fresh horse
will take the mail and hustle it on. Day and night, rain or
shine, they'll keep that mail moving. Same way with eastbound mail out of California."

Jeff was leaning forward over the table. His eyes shone,
the knuckles of his clenched hands were white. Chet was
outwardly calm, but suppressed excitement was in his voice:

"Have they hired all their riders yet?"

"I don't know for sure, but I think they have them pretty
well lined up by this time. They arranged for board and
rooms here at the Patee House for a bunch of the fellows
they've hired—that's why I'm here. I don't usually live
quite this high—" his quizzical glance flicked the ornate tables, "but the company is paying the bills, and I'll
try anything once. It won't be much like this out on the
trail."

"Does your uncle do the hiring here?"

"He took on two or three fellows. Mr. Majors has hired
most of them here on the east end, I think—he and Mr.
Russell."

"Do you reckon we could get on?" Jeff demanded.

"I couldn't say for sure, Jeff. Hard to tell. Have you
boys done much riding?"

"Been at it all our lives. Dad said I was five when he
started me out on my first pony." Quick memories of child-
hood, of an understanding father, rose before Jeff. He

9

winked, swallowed hard. "I can ride anything they trot out, and Chet's better'n I am," he declared earnestly.

Alex's appraising glance took them both in. "You'd be old enough, I guess," he said to Chet. Then, as he looked again at Jeff: "How old are you?"

"I'll be seventeen in July. He's only a year and about nine months older'n I am!"

"Most of the fellows they've hired are around twenty, or older. But I don't know that there's any hard and fast age limit. Tell you what I'll do—my uncle went to Denver, but I expect him back on the next stage. I'll tell him about you two, and get him to give me a note for you to give Mr. Majors, and if there's any chance—"

"I wish you would!" Both eager listeners spoke at once.

"I will. It may not work, but no harm to try."

They had finished the last morsels of the last course; the colored boy, from a little distance, was plainly waiting for them to go. "I guess this is about all of it, fellows," Alex said, dryly.

As they walked down a corridor, the thin, sweet note of a violin floated to them above the strumming of the wind outside. Jeff, a step behind Chet and Alex, caught a glimpse, through a door ajar, of a big room, a bare, polished floor, and a group of white-clad girls standing in one corner. Only a glimpse, as he hurried along after the two leading the way. Several incoming youths, wearing red shirts, blue trousers, and high glossy boots, brushed in past them with easy assurance at the outer door, talking, laughing, exchanging familiar greetings with Alex.

"A bunch of the riders. That's the Pony Express uniform they've got on," Alex explained, as the trio went out onto the dimly lighted street. "It's a better rig for dancing, I guess, than for riding trail. They're having a dance here tonight."

The wind, now risen, hit them fair as they moved away from the shelter of the great hotel. It was blowing from the west, a savage wind, bearing the scent of far, wild spaces.

Westward in the darkness lay the wildest stretches of an untamed continent. Six hundred miles of prairie, where roamed the Indian and the buffalo. Then, rising from the high plains, the great mountain barrier. Hundreds of miles of snow-blown peaks and barren, wind-whipped plateaus. Beyond, stark deserts, wherein whole rivers sank and vanished forever. Beyond all this, the jagged, pine-clad Sierra Nevadas, from whose westering slopes gold-bearing canyons opened and widened into valleys descending to the Golden Gate.

Like a living presence, the poignant mystery and luring challenge of the West pressed on Jeff, ever more imaginative and sensitive than his brother. Hope and longing keyed him. "If you'll only help us get on as riders for the Pony Express, we—we'll never forget it," he urged Alex.

"I'll do what I can," said their new-found friend. "But don't bank too strong on it. They're liable to have all the places filled by now. Where you fellows going to stop tonight?"

"Hadn't figured that out yet," Chet answered. "Most any place will do us."

"If you don't object to taking a bunk in a cabin, I know a place down here on the bottom—won't cost you a cent."

"Just the thing. If you'll show us where it is, we'll sure appreciate it."

11

II ON!

Chet and Jeff might have gone by with only a glance at the wooden saddle swinging overhead, but the square of roughly lettered brown paper in the big wooden frame stopped them in front of the shop of Israel Landis.

> *We'll have you know*
> *Our saddles go*
> *Through all the West, from old St. Joe.*
> *In any weather*
> *Squeeze our leather.*
> *It's so good there is none better.*

They read it twice, this sample of the weekly renewed "saddle poetry" that was known and repeated by riders on more than one lonely western trail.

"Old Israel's got plenty to do right now, anyway," commented a stranger who noticed their interest, "making all them saddles and fixings for the Pony Express line Alex Majors is going to start."

"Say, I'd like to see one of those Express saddles," Jeff exclaimed. "Do they care if folks go in and take a look?"

"Of course not. Go ahead."

The noted saddlery's long room was lined with work benches and busy workmen. The brothers sighted a saddle of odd appearance on a rack near the front door and stepped closer to see it better.

It had a shorter horn and a lower cantle than the stock saddles they were used to riding. It was short-skirted; the rosaderos were scanty and the light-weight stirrups had no tapaderas, yet it looked sturdy and roomy.

As they stood there an apprentice about Jeff's age came along, with friendly grin.

"Is this what they're going to use on the Pony Express?" Chet asked.

"That's the job, right there. What d'you think of it?"

"Nice work, but somehow it looks like it wasn't quite all there."

"Well, of course the mochila fits on over that." The apprentice went to a rack farther back, and returned with a big square of leather on his arm. With a deft swing, he slipped this over the saddle. It went neatly into place, covering the whole saddle except the horn and the cantle, which stuck up through openings cut for them. On the mochila's wide skirt were four compartments of hard leather, two on each side, one in front and one behind each stirrup, fitted with small brass padlocks. Snug-fitting, smartly tooled, the

13

russet-leather mochila matched the saddle perfectly, and completed it.

"Now how do you like it?" asked the apprentice.

"Say, that's mighty slick!" Jeff did not try to hide his admiration. "I reckon the little pockets are for the letters?"

"Yep, the mail goes in them cantinas; that's the name for 'em, Spanish, I reckon. You see, this mochila goes clean through, all the way to California. When they change horses at a station they'll have the fresh horse saddled beforehand, so when the rider gets in all he'll have to do is jerk off the mochila and slap it onto the other saddle. Save a minute or two at every station. Quite a scheme, ain't it?"

"Say, it sure is!"

More than Alex Carlyle's account, more than the comments rife along the streets of St. Joseph, this smart, specially designed saddle made the Pony Express a living thing to the two boys. Chet made no outward sign. Jeff drew a long breath, his hands unconsciously clenched.

"Come on back here and I'll show you the tree we use on this job," the apprentice invited.

Chet shook his head. "Thanks, but we'll have to be moving along. Got to see a man on business. Maybe we'll drop in again some day."

They hurried to the express office on Second Street, eying with fresh respect the gilded sign in front:

RUSSELL, MAJORS & WADDELL

The man behind the plank counter hardly glanced up at these persistent callers.

"Is Mister Majors in now?" Jeff asked.

"Just got here. Knock on that door." He waved a hand toward a closed door at the rear of the room.

They crossed the floor with light tread and tapped on the door.

"Come in," called a deep voice. Hats in hand, the boys swung the door partly back, slipped through, and closed it behind them.

Alexander Majors confronted them across a flat-topped desk.

Young as Chet and Jeff were, they needed no one to tell them that here was a man of importance. They instantly sensed distinction in that commanding, almost imperious face, with straight, handsome nose and direct, dark eyes that matched the black mustache and trimmed beard.

Alexander Majors, "the Kentucky Christian who never drank and never swore," was a noted man in the West. His far-reaching freighting and contracting enterprises, carried on first singly and later with partners, his high integrity, and just treatment of employees were known from the Missouri River to the Pacific Coast.

"What is it?" he now inquired.

The envelope that had been in Chet's inner pocket had found its way into his hands without his knowing it. "Mr. Ficklin told us to present this to you, sir," he said, holding it out. "Alex Carlyle, Mr. Ficklin's nephew, is a friend of ours, sir."

Majors tore the envelope, read the note in a glance, and gave Chet a longer look. "What can I do for you?"

"Well, sir, just as soon as we heard about the Pony Express, we wondered what chance there'd be of our working for you, riding. We know how to ride, and how to handle a horse to get the most out of him without killing him off. And we're neither one of us too heavy for long-distance riding."

Majors scanned the two boys with the keen glance that had sized up countless men. He noted their steady eyes, their square-set jaws, the lightly poised way they stood. Then his gaze fixed on Chet. "Weigh about a hundred thirty, don't you?" he commented.

"Just about that. Yes, sir."

"That's a good weight, not too much, and you look as though it were all muscle. What's your idea if you got a job, to work a month or two and then quit and drift into something else? If that's it, better not try to get on. We want riders who will stick."

Chet considered. "Mr. Majors," he said, earnestly, "if you'll take us on, I promise you we'll stay with it. We aim to play fair with anybody that gives us half a chance. We've seen several of the fellows who are going to ride the Express, and we're pretty sure we can fit in with the outfit. I wish you'd try us, sir."

"We have enough men now to get the thing started," Majors replied, "and have turned down a lot of applicants. But Ficklin told me this morning he could use one more good man, if I cared to take another one on. You look like a chap who can be depended on. I'll give you a chance."

"But I want on, too!" Jeff stepped closer to the desk, his face eager, his eyes bright. "We always go together, Chet and me!"

"Pony Express riders will work alone, not in pairs," said

16

Majors. "We can use only one more at present. You look rather young for this, anyhow."

"I'll be seventeen in July! He's not so much older than I am!"

"I can use one, no more. Sorry, but that's the way it is. If you do not care to go ahead with it—" he glanced at Chet —"there are plenty of fellows who will."

Finality was in his voice; his manner, as he reached for a paper on his desk, showed that there would be no debate on the matter.

Jeff's lips set in a straighter line. He moved his lithe shoulders suddenly as though to throw off a weight. He stepped close to Chet. "Go ahead," he whispered. "Don't miss this chance. Go on." He almost shoved his brother forward.

"I'll take it, sir," Chet said, quietly.

Majors slid open a drawer of his desk and took out a slip of paper. "Read the Express rider's oath and see if you have any objections to it."

Chet read it intently. Jeff eyed it with him. "No, sir, that is all right with me."

"If you ride for us, Harlowe, I want you to understand what this enterprise is. It isn't just a matter of seeing how fast and how far a string of good horses can go. It isn't just a matter of trying to make money—we want to make something out of it if we can, but the expenses and risks will be so great that we are more likely to lose money. The Pony Express is being formed to bind the East and West more closely together. Quick communication makes for union. America has expanded with a giant's stride in the last few

17

years. She now is imperial in extent. If she can only stay united she will, under God's providence, become the greatest nation the sun ever shone on.

"If you ride for the Pony Express you will have a hard part in a big undertaking. In a very real way you will be a courier of empire. Do you want on?"

Chet's pulse quickened. He listened strangely to his own voice. "Yes, sir, I do."

Majors, leaning over in his chair, took a small red-edged book from a lower drawer. A motion of his head then drew Chet closer. Majors stood up. "Put your left hand on the Bible," he directed. "Raise your right hand, and repeat the words after me."

Jeff stood back. He watched the slanting shaft of spring sunlight on the pine boards, he listened to the two voices, phrase by phrase:

"I, Chester Harlowe, do hereby swear before the great and living God that during my engagement, and while I am an employee of Russell, Majors, and Waddell, I will under no circumstances use profane language; that I will drink no intoxicating liquors; that I will not quarrel or fight with other employees of the firm, and that in every respect I will conduct myself honestly, be faithful to my duties, and so direct all my acts as to win the confidence of my employers. So help me God."

Majors laid the printed oath on the desk. He handed Chet a pen. "You may sign that."

Chet took the pen in rope-hard fingers and carefully wrote his name.

Jeff, watching, thrilled. His hair prickled. Something

bright and quick, seen only of the inward eye, moved before him in the small, plain room. The slanting sunlight on the desk was suddenly a strong hand, pointing to hard ways. A prevision of trouble touched him uncannily.

"Now you are a part of the Pony Express organization," Majors was saying in a matter-of-fact tone to Chet. He wrote hastily on a slip of paper. "Take this to Brown and Blake, on Fourth Street. They will fix you up with a uniform. You will stay at the Patee House until assigned to a station. B. F. Ficklin will make the assignments and give you detailed instructions. I wish you success."

"Thank you, sir," Chet replied. He and Jeff withdrew to the outer office, and the street.

The Patee House had no equal in all the West in size and appointments. It had opened with glorious fanfare in 1858. Within a year the new Hannibal & St. Joseph Railroad located its depot not near by, as had been counted on by John Patee, but seven blocks away from the new hotel. The current of business began setting toward the railroad and away from the Patee House. The grand lobby with its shining columns and oil paintings, the elaborate cuisine, could not make up for the hotel's bad location. Misfortune and loss attended the efforts of each of the various managers who strove, one after another, to make a success of this ill-starred hostelry.

Chet and Jeff knew nothing about the ill-fortune that was beginning to settle upon the place. The big lobby was grand to them, and at any other time would have been almost awesome, but this day nothing could have stopped them. They stalked boldly up the steps. Their high boot heels thumped across the polished floor. Jeff, a half-step behind his brother, noticed now that the gilt paint was flaking away from the base of one of the big columns. Chet gave the dapper desk clerk a level look.

"Mr. Majors sent me here," he announced, shifting his grasp on the long pasteboard box that held his uniform. "I'm a Pony Express rider."

The clerk shoved the big register around. "Put your name down there," he directed, loftily. "I'll see what we have." He gave Jeff a questioning look.

"My brother is going up with me for a little while," Chet said, firmly.

"Here, boy!" called the clerk, to a gangling negro lad who had shuffled into view. "Take these gentlemen up to three sixteen."

Chet had tried on his uniform before taking it from the store, but now, in the unaccustomed luxury and privacy of his own hotel room, he hastened to try it on again. Jeff stood by silently. When the change was made, Chet turned to survey himself in the long mirror. Red shirt, blue trousers, high shiny boots, neat dark cap! He drew himself still straighter; pride shone in his face. A rider for the Pony Express!

In the mirror, as he looked, then, he glimpsed Jeff's face, pale, twisting with a spasm of soundless grief, turning instantly away lest he be seen.

Chet swung around. Jeff was looking out of the window, his back turned to his brother.

Chet walked over to him, laid his hand on his arm, pulled

him around. Jeff winked fast, a tear escaped and ran down his cheek; he tried to pull away, fighting to control himself.

"Look here! I won't go if that's the way you feel about it, Jeff. I'll turn this thing in and let 'em keep it. The old Pony Express ain't the only outfit in the world! We'll look around and get some job where we'll be together!"

Jeff's eyes blazed. He managed to steady his voice. "Just you try it! You back out, Chester Harlowe, and I'm done with you! The Harlowes gettin' to be quitters, are they? You stick! D'you hear me?"

His manner carried conviction. Chet looked vastly relieved. "Well, if you think I better," he yielded. "But if you say the word, I'll let this thing go, and we can stay together."

"You're on, now, and you're going to stay on," Jeff returned, firmly. He was master of destiny in that moment, was almost master of his own feelings. He swung again to face the window.

"Lemme have your bowie knife a minute, Chet," he said, his voice elaborately casual. "I want to trim this old flapper off the sole o' my boot."

III   THE MAIL STARTS

EAGER crowds filled the streets, the eating houses, and the trading places of St. Joseph on April 3, 1860. Something in the air that day stirred faintly even the dullest; those sensitive and alert thrilled with high emotion. The continent, still unsubdued, scarcely explored, was that day being made smaller. The vast, silent prairies, over which still lingered the desert legend, the mysterious intermountain land of the Mormons, the golden Western coast—all were that day being bound closer together. The flying hoofs of the best horses and the nerve of the best riders in all the West were to work the miracle. The Pony Express—audacious American exploit—ten days from the Missouri River to the Golden Gate!

Jeff, thrilling to the excitement, stuck to his job on the

22

dray line, bending his back to heavy loads all day. A poor job, and one that he knew would last no longer than that week. But he stuck till at last quitting time came. Then he hurried to the Express Company's stable, south of Patee Park, fearing he would be too late, expecting every moment to hear the signal announcing that the Pony Express had started.

A crowd was milling aimlessly in the street in front of the stable. The stable doors were shut. Jeff pressed through the throng and pounded on the doors. "Alex!" he called. "Let me in, will you?"

A door opened slightly, he squeezed through, then the door was barred again.

"What's the matter, Alex?" he demanded. "Haven't they started yet? It's way after five o'clock."

"The train's late! Don't know how much. They can't go till it gets in, it's bringing Eastern mail for the Express."

"Who's going to ride? You?"

"We drew straws for it—Billy Richardson won." Alex fought down a cough. "Come on back and see the layout. He's going to ride that brown mare that took your eye the other day."

Back in a box stall, knee-deep in straw, several lithe, bronzed lads were grouped around a slim, high-spirited brown mare. They wore the fancy red shirts, blue trousers, and high boots of Pony Express riders.

The brown mare whinnied impatiently as the hostlers, feeding the other horses along the manger rows, passed her by; the red-shirted riders waited tensely. For the twentieth time, Billy Richardson examined and adjusted the creaking

23

new Express saddle. Seven o'clock now, soft April dusk creeping into the stalls, faintly heard notes coming from Rosenblatt's Brass Band, playing to the crowds uptown.

"You're all dressed up, Billy," Alex chaffed.

Richardson grinned. "Yes, but you know how it is, if the crowd doesn't." He fingered the silver bugle at his belt. "This bugle, and these fancy chaps—" he shook his wolf-skin chaps impatiently, "are all for show. I'll leave 'em on the ferryboat as I go over. Just about as well leave 'em here, be so dark pretty quick nobody uptown'll see 'em anyhow." He straightened his slim, muscular figure. "This," he patted the Colt revolver in his holster, "goes with me. But there's precious little chance for danger on this first lap. The country across the river is getting pretty well settled up for the first fifty miles. The fun with the Indians will all be further west. I wish—"

"Listen!" Alex interrupted.

Faint, but clear, a whistle sounded. The special train was coming at last!

Richardson sprang into the saddle. The incoming mail had yet to be rushed from the train to the Express office, wrapped in oiled silk to keep out moisture, and locked in the mochila before the starting signal would sound, but he was not going to have any of the delay charged to him. The brown mare pressed up to the closed stable doors and thrust nervously at the bit.

The whistle sounded again, loudly. Then silence, more waiting, while the slow dusk thickened.

Boom! The jarring report of a cannon, blocks away, gave the signal. Impatient hands flung the stable doors wide open.

Shouts warned the crowd outside: "Get back!" "Look out!" "Here he comes!"

With a farewell wave of his hand for those in the stable, Richardson dashed out. Around a corner and down a street he sped to the Express office. There he swung out of the saddle while the mochila with its padlocked cantinas was fitted into place. Then he leaped again to his seat and galloped through gathering darkness, along streets filled with waving, yelling men, to the foot of Jule Street, and clattered up the gangplank of the waiting ferryboat *Denver*.

Jeff, watching from the stable door, lost sight of him as he rounded the corner. Jeff stood there a little time listening to the rising and falling cheers that marked the rider's swift flight to the ferry. He looked about, then, for Alex Carlyle. But Alex had gone, as had the other Pony Express riders. The crowd had melted away. From inside the stable came the muted sounds of evening—the rattle of halters, the stamp of hoofs, a low, steady munching along the rows of feed boxes. Loneliness pressed upon Jeff. He thought of Chet, with pride, yet with a stabbing thrust of longing, gone now a week to his station on the Pony Express line far out on the high plains, somewhere west of Julesburg.

Hard to bear, this separation. Hard likewise for Jeff was the knowledge that though the first Pony Express was now speeding gloriously into the night and the West, he himself had no part in it. Yet his shoulders were squared, his head was up, his lips were a thin, straight line as he turned and walked slowly down the dark, silent street.

"Mister, what's the chance for a job?"

The tall, hatchet-faced proprietor of the livery and sale stable looked Jeff up and down before he spoke. "Know anything about horses?"

"Yes, sir, I've worked with them quite a lot."

"Have, eh? Do you reckon you could ride a pony down to the water trough for me?"

"Sure. Where's the pony?"

"Back here in the corral." The man, with a wink and a motion of the head which escaped Jeff, led the way through the long, low stable. Jeff followed close. A couple of men who had been squatting on their heels in front of the stable got up and walked after them.

Inside the pole corral a mud-caked calico mustang stood tied to a post.

The man hauled a stock saddle and a bridle out of a feed trough. The ewe-necked mustang stood with drooping head and drawn-back ears while he slipped the bridle on, settled the saddle in place, and drew up the latigos.

Jeff turned and laid his small bundle of clothing in the feed trough. As he did, he met the glance of one of the two men perched on the top rail of the corral, and fancied he caught, in an almost imperceptible motion of the fellow's head, a signal of warning.

He stepped closer to the jug-headed mustang. He saw it had a wicked eye on him; he sensed something vicious beneath the brute's docile stand.

"Ready?" asked the man.

"Yep."

He went up with a quick, light swing. His right foot caught its stirrup at the first thrust.

26

The mustang's head jerked down as Jeff hit the saddle, its withers came up, its back humped till the saddle crawled. Straight up in the air it went, coming down stiff-legged. It hit the gravel like a ton of brick. It shot across the corral in twisting, hard-hitting jumps, muscles bunched like steel coils. The saddle strings snapped like whiplashes.

Jeff was there. He was part of the saddle. His left hand gripped the reins, his right swung his hat in wide circles. "E-yah! Whoopee!" he yelled.

The mustang threw itself on its side. Jeff slipped free of the saddle as the mud-caked brute went down, crouched beside it as it lay for an instant kicking, and swung into the saddle as it jumped to its feet. It plunged for the corral wall to scrape him off, but he twitched its head around and swung it into the clear.

Now the mustang lunged, leaped crookedly, with arched back and closely gathered feet. Gravel sprayed the corral walls. Jeff was dizzy. Sky, earth, and corral were one blur to him. He stuck.

One more frantic burst of bucking, then the mustang straightened out into easy crowhops. It swung to the rein; Jeff brought it around and rode it up to the corral gate, where it stood, trembling, foam-covered. "Nice pony you've got, mister," he grinned to the tall man perched on the top rail of the corral. "Where'd you say that water trough is?"

"Boy, you're a rider!" The man dropped to the ground inside the corral. "I 'lowed you'd last just about two jumps. The joke is on me. So you're looking for a job? Say, if I had anything at all I could give you to do, I'd take you on, but I hain't got a thing, right now."

27

He was loosening the latigos as he talked. Jeff picked his bundle out of the trough, then, turning away, met again the eye of the man who had caught his attention before he climbed into the saddle. This time the motion of the man's head was unmistakable. Jeff walked over to where he was standing apart in the corral.

This man stood arrow-straight in fringed, weathered buckskin. His sun-darkened face was smooth, save for a long mustache. Hardness showed in his lean features and cold eyes. His hair hung to the shoulders of his jacket. A rifle was slung across his back; Jeff noted the queer glitter of its short barrel.

Seeing his interest, the man slipped the gun strap and held the rifle out for inspection. He spoke charily: "I've got 'er cased."

Jeff took the gun and looked closely. "What's it cased with?"

"Skin uv a bull snake."

"Oh!"

"Yep. Nice ridin'."

"Thanks. I was lucky, I reckon."

"Rode plenty, probably."

"Well, yes, sir. Father started me in the saddle when I was just a little shaver. We always had lots of horses—I rode 'em all. Used to break horses for our neighbors."

Again the cold eyes measured Jeff. "Lookin' fur a job?"

"Yes, sir, I am. Had a job here in town on a dray line, but the man sold out, and the new outfit had their own men."

"I kin use a rider."

"What sort of work is it, mister?"

28

"Rounding up wild horses. You rope?"

"Just a little—I'm not very good at it."

"Me an' my partner kin do the roping. We had another fellow. He pulled out."

"Did you say you wanted to hire somebody? How long would the job last?"

" 'Bout a month. No wages. I'll furnish horses an' grub, you kin have a sixth of what we ketch. Might have luck, might not. Last trip we got eight, fetched about six hundred dollars."

Jeff checked his first impulse. "How soon would you have to know?" he asked, then. "I'll have to see a friend of mine first. If I let you know this afternoon will that do?"

"Yep. I'll be around here, likely. If you don't see me ask 'em where Bill Sanderson is."

Jeff slipped through the gate and started away, then turned back. "Where is it you go to catch the horses?" he asked.

"This side o' the Cimarron, mostly."

"Thanks, Mister Sanderson." Jeff hurried off.

He encountered Alex Carlyle coming down the steps at the main entrance of the Patee House, and drew him aside. "What do you think about it?" he demanded, after relating his talk with Sanderson.

Alex pondered, leaning against the entrance railing. A flush not from the burning May sun showed in his thin cheeks. He looked frail beside Jeff.

"I believe I'd try it, if I were you," he said. "You're in shape to stand hard knocks, I reckon, Jeff? You want to be, if you trail with a bunch of horse hunters."

"That ain't the part that bothers me. I—you know the thing I'm after is to get on the Pony Express. Chet's on, and I won't be satisfied till I'm hooked up with the same outfit he is. But I can't go in every day asking them for a riding job—I've bothered Mr. Majors and your uncle, too, till I'm most ashamed to face them again, for a little while, anyway. But I've got to be doing *something*. Do you reckon I'd lose out entirely with the Pony Express if I throw in with this horse-hunting outfit for a few weeks?"

"I don't think so," Alex averred. "My guess is there'll be chances to get on the Express after a little, when some of the new wears off. Some of these riders will get tired of the job, or maybe get sick. I didn't feel any too good myself when I got in with the mail yesterday," he admitted, with a good-natured grimace.

Jeff gave him a glance of friendly concern, in silence.

"Another thing," Alex went on; "this man Sanderson is a top hand on trail. Everybody knows him. If you make good with his outfit it'll show you sure can ride—might help you getting on afterward. Of course you'd be taking a chance, you might not make a thing chasing horses. But most everybody takes a chance once in a while."

"Sure, I reckon that's right."

"You might say this whole Pony Express business is just chance-taking on a big scale. The Express Company hasn't got any government contract for carrying the mail. Senator Gwin of California talked Mr. Russell into believing that the Postmaster General would give the company a contract later on, after they had set up fast mail service to the coast over the central route. Mr. Majors didn't think much of that way of doing business, neither did Mr. Waddell, but Russell had given his word to try it, and they backed him up. They may make some money, and they may lose a lot. That's the way I got the line-up from my uncle."

"Well, I reckon I can take a chance, too," Jeff decided, soberly. He looked at Alex, and Alex as gravely looked at him. "That man said the outfit was going 'this side of the Cimarron,'" Jeff added. "What is the Cimarron? Where is it?"

"A river, southwest of here. Starts out on the plains somewhere and runs down into the Indian Country."

"First time I ever heard of it," Jeff mused.

Uneasy silence, then, till Alex spoke. "Well, here's luck, old man."

"Same to you." Jeff gripped the thin hand with his sinewy fingers. "I'll look you up first thing when I get back. You'll still be on the Pony Express, of course?"

"Sure. Sure thing."

Bill Sanderson, his partner Tod Albee, and Jeff crossed the Missouri on the ferry's first trip next morning. Their remuda of fifteen ponies trailed on lead ropes. Saddlebags and two pack ponies carried their supplies—a pup tent, blankets, lariats, hackamores, clogs, grass hobbles, a mess kit, hardtack, bacon, beans, and coffee. Sanderson's snake-cased rifle was in his saddle boot; each rider wore a Colt's revolver in a holster tied down with a strip of rawhide. They trooped down the *Denver's* gangplank with a clatter, crossed the wide bottom on the Kansas side of the river, topped the bluffs and headed southwest.

31

They camped that night far beyond the lonely ranches that dotted the first twenty-five or thirty miles beyond the river.

Jeff woke next morning wondering where he was. The weathered side of the tent was hanging against his face; through the raised flap he caught the wild, sweet smell of the plains. Then his brain cleared; he rolled out of his blanket, stiff and saddle-sore. Tod Albee had a clear fire of buffalo chips going in front of the tent; coffee was in the pot, bacon in the blackened frying pan. Sanderson was coming in from the picket line. Jeff, watching him, caught the half-grin that creased his face and felt all at once at home.

Hours later Jeff swung his pony closer to Albee's; spoke above the beat of hoofs: "What's that yonder?"

Albee's distance-set eyes, narrowed against the westering sun, had seen the dark splotch minutes before.

"Buffalo."

The splotch widened; tiny dots showed on its borders. Only keen eyes, noting from time to time, could see that it moved. It lay northwestward on a far ridge and slowly grew more distant as the remuda kept its steady trot.

"Was that a big herd?" Jeff asked.

"No. Maybe a thousand head."

Always ahead on the rolling horizon lay a divide. Jeff at first supposed that when he got to the top of a ridge he would be able to see as far as his eyes could carry. Always, instead, he saw ahead of him another crest, like a wave in a brown-green sea. The short curly buffalo grass was soft beneath the ponies' feet. The flowers of springtime were in bloom.

32

They topped a ridge late in the fifth day and looked out upon a basin, ringed miles wide with higher ground. A group of dots showed on the basin floor. "There's horses," Albee said.

Sanderson scanned the dots with field glasses while the tired remuda stood. His glance roved the nearer side of the basin. "Looks like water yonder," he decided, and swung his pony.

They camped beside a tiny creek bed fringed with dwarfed willows. Sanderson turned in as soon as supper was over. Tod Albee lounged on the curly grass beside the graying campfire. Jeff lingered with him. The ponies grazed on the picket line. The wind was down; the stars blazed clear.

"How do you go at it catching wild horses, Tod? Can't they outrun our ponies?"

"Probably can. But there's a way. Say you and I was to ride out toward this bunch ahead of us here. It looks like about a dozen head, probably a stallion, five or six mares, and some colts or yearlings. They'd see us, see we were strange. Away goes the whole outfit on the run, the stallion driving 'em ahead of him."

"Then what would we do?"

"Ride after 'em. Keep 'em moving all day. Here's the thing of it—horses hate to leave the range they're used to. They'll run from us, but after they go ten or fifteen miles they'll circle back and probably come around within a couple of miles of where they started from. That gives us a chance to hustle over and grab a fresh pony and a bite to eat. Then we got to hurry and catch up with 'em again. Keep 'em on the move till about dark, then let 'em drift, and watch with glasses to see where they settle down. We may have to back-track a little—if we stayed too close our ponies might whinny to 'em and start the whole bunch off again."

"Then we come back to camp?"

"Nope, stay right there. Use your saddle for a pillow. Hobble your pony. Wrap up in your saddle blanket."

"And start after them again in the morning?"

"Sure, the next day, and same way for maybe four or five days. Keep a-going, changing ponies right along. By that time the herd'll be so tired you can get in close. Then you can turn 'em, make 'em travel in a circle.

"After a while the weaker ones will just stand and let the others swing around 'em—that's milling. When they've been milled till they're dog-tired, rope 'em and put the clogs on. Takes three hands for that, one ropes, one handles the clogs, and one drives the rest of the herd off a little ways. . . . We'd better get some sleep while we've got a chance."

JEFF, making his slow way to the ferry, wondered that the *Denver's* stack and pilot house showed above the tall weeds that hid the river from him. His high-heeled boots plopped in the thick dust as he strode along. The weeds and brush that fringed the bottom trail were gray with dust. The very air was dusty. The grass in the wayside glades was withered. Big cracks crisscrossed the iron-hard earth.

But when he got in sight of the landing he saw that the Missouri was booming. Its brown flood swirled only a little below the top of the cut bank. The *Denver's* nose was against the bank; outfits were embarking across the level gangplank. A couple of empty freight wagons, drawn by ox teams, a weathered emigrant rig, eastbound, several men on horseback. He walked on and stood by the rail.

A bell jingled, the boat backed out, swung, and headed for the St. Joe side. The coffee-colored eddies of the great stream took the massive boat as lightly as a chip. Scarred, barkless tree trunks were slipping by in midchannel, jagged spurs of limbs showing as they rolled over in the swift current.

"She's a-boiling, ain't she?" said one man to another, close to Jeff.

"Yep. Old June raise. Always comes."

Jeff hurried ashore as soon as the gangplank touched the Jule Street wharf. He hastened up the hill with only one backward glance at the wide river rolling somber and brown under the June sun. He clumped along sun-blistered wooden sidewalks to the Patee House.

The wide hotel lobby was cool and dark. The tall columns, the polished floor, the picture-hung walls, contrasting with the hard, empty prairie spaces over which he had been riding, awed him again. He paused to get his bearings.

The murmur of talk came to him; he looked across to a group of men standing in a corner. He listened to a heated voice: "I repeat, suh, slavery is a sacred institution. You Northerners do not understand it. Better for you to keep your hands off it, suh. We don't propose to have any rail-splitting politician from Illinois tell us what to do with our own property! Arguments may be well enough, but here, suh, is the sentiment of the state of Kentucky: *When the argument is exhausted, we will stand by our arms!*"

Another voice, lower, made a reply he could not hear clearly. The first speaker's rejoinder sounded loud: "Ready? Every true Southerner is ready to meet the issue, suh, any time, anywhere!"

Jeff overcame his reluctance and walked up to the desk. He felt dusty and out of place under the gaze of the dapper clerk. "Is Mr. Alex Carlyle here in the hotel?" he asked.

"Hasn't been here for several weeks," said the clerk, turning away decisively.

Jeff waited uncertainly, then retreated, doing his best to walk noiselessly in high-heeled boots. Near the door he wheeled as he caught sight of a rough-and-ready sort of man. In two strides he was at the man's side. "How do you do, Mr. Ficklin?" he ventured.

"Well, hello, there! Haven't seen you lately."

"No, sir, I've been out West, after wild horses."

"Have, eh? Just get back?"

"Yes, sir, just got in last night." Darkness from Ficklin's mood seemed to flow out over him. "How—how is the Pony Express going, sir? Where is Alex these days?"

"Alex is in bad shape. His folks came and took him home." Ficklin shook his head gloomily.

"Alex sick! Why, he was riding regular when I left here. What's the matter with him, Mr. Ficklin?"

"Lung trouble of the worst sort. The doctor says there's hardly a chance for him." Ficklin, looking at Jeff, seemed to question, then to decide. "You just got in, you say. Have you heard about your brother?"

"No, sir, I was going to ask you about him, but I hardly reckoned you'd know—he's away out the other side of Julesburg, and—"

Ficklin's hand on Jeff's shoulder. Foreboding touching Jeff in the same instant. "He—he's not—"

"Steady, now, Jeff. It may turn out all right. Your brother got shot. Four or five days ago. A holdup. They

37

took him in to Julesburg. Rider brought the word in here last night. I don't know just how bad he was hit, but he's young and in good shape, so he'll probably pull through."

Jeff stood still, his old hat crumpled tight in his hands, his face pale under its deep tan.

"Yes, it's bad," Ficklin said. "Everything is going wrong just now. The Indians have been on a rampage west of Salt Lake. Burned a lot of stations, stole the horses or drove them off, killed a stationman or two. Nobody can get through. Our last California mail got in here June first—eleven days ago. We're sending mail out of here, but only as far west as Salt Lake City.

"The Express isn't going to quit, is it?"

"Not much! We don't do business that way. We'll get these Indians out of the way in a few days. When we get lined up again we're going to run the Express twice a week."

Jeff seemed scarcely to hear him. "Stage is running between here and Julesburg, is it?" he asked, quietly.

"Yes."

"I better get out there, I reckon."

"I don't know as that's necessary," said Ficklin, kindly. "They'll do whatever they can for your brother, just the same."

"I reckon I better go."

"Well, I expect I'd feel that way if I was in your place. Wouldn't do any harm. . . . I'll have to be going, Jeff. Hope things turn out all right."

He was turning away, but Jeff had one more question. "They didn't say whereabouts Chet was hit, did they?"

"No, Jeff, they didn't. They just said somebody tried to

hold up the mail. Your brother got through and brought the mail with him, but he got hit." Ficklin turned away. Jeff stole out of the ornate lobby.

In the glare and heat of outdoors, he felt freer. He walked first to the Express office, found that the fare to Julesburg was fifty dollars, that a stage was starting west the next day. Then, finding Sanderson at the same livery stable where he had first encountered the horse hunter, he sold out for seventy-five dollars his share in the horses they had caught.

There then was nothing more for him to do. The June day seemed endless as he roved the streets of St. Joseph.

The afternoon sun was drawing great blobs of resin from the pine sidewalk as he stopped under the wooden awning of a false-fronted grocery store. Careless at first of the talk of the loungers in this spot of shade, he roused quickly to attention:

"I reckon Alex Majors ain't a-cutting quite as big a swath with his Pony Express as he figured on."

"I dunno, what about it, anyhow?"

"They hain't been ary rider in from California fur purty nigh two weeks. Guess the Indians busted the thing up. That was a fool idea anyhow, I could 'uv told 'em that before ever they started. Trying to carry mail two thousand miles a-hossback! 'Twon't work, I tell you. A good stage line, now, that's the way to get mail through. Butterfield's line is makin' its schedule right along—see by the paper this morning she landed on time at St. Louis, and brought the California dispatches with 'er."

"I dunno but what you're right. Even supposing they *could* make it on horseback in summertime, winter would sure stop 'em. Never make it through South Pass. I reckon for once old Majors has bit off more'n he can chaw."

Jeff checked the angry remonstrance that rose to his lips. But he would not listen to a decrial of the Pony Express. He stalked angrily away through the blistering sunlight.

About half-past five that afternoon, he was standing at the foot of Jule Street. The *Denver* lay there, her idle gangplank resting on the battered timbers of the wharf. The day's rush was over.

Far and faint, the note of a bugle sounded on the hot air. Jeff looked across a half-mile of brown water to the landing on the other side. There, close to the edge of the cut bank, stood a horse and rider. The sunlight flashed on something bright, the bugle sounded again.

A bell jingled on the *Denver*. Deck hands cast off the heavy hawser. Another bell. The boat backed, swung, and went slogging out into the stream, her nose pointing up to offset the swift current.

Jeff waited while she made the round trip. As the boat stood in to the Jule Street landing he recognized the rider. Johnny Fry, on a black horse, with a Pony Express mochila on his saddle.

"Hi, Jeff!" the rider called, waving his hand, as he clattered down the gangplank.

"How's everything, Johnny?"

"Fine! Come on down to the stable." Johnny forced the foam-covered black to a gallop, heading for the Express office on Second Street.

Jeff hurried a long mile to the company stable, south of Patee Park. He found the stable doors open and went on down the rows of stalls till he caught the glint of Johnny's beaded Indian jacket. Johnny thought first of the mail, next of his horse. Everything else could wait. He was talking to the negro hostler.

"Don't let him have more than a swallow or two of water for an hour, anyhow. Let him cool off. I pushed him, and it's mighty hot."

"All right, suh."

"And be sure to rub him down good."

"Yas, suh, ah'll tend to him right. Jes leave it to me."

"Did you hear anything about Chet—my brother?" Jeff demanded. "He got shot, you know—holdup, west of Julesburg."

"I asked Bob Lee—Bob brought the mail into Granada," Johnny replied. "He said they reported to him your brother was holding his own pretty good."

"That all he said?"

"Well, yes—you know it's a long ways out there, and a lot of riders passing the word along. I thought I was lucky to get any word at all, Jeff."

"Do you reckon there's a doctor out at Julesburg, Johnny?"

"I don't know. Don't suppose so. But of course there might be, at that. Sure, there might be."

"What's the news from out West?" Jeff asked, as they walked toward the door.

"Well, this pouch I brought in came from Ruby Valley. That's three hundred miles west of Salt Lake City. The whole shebang from Ruby Valley west to the Sierras has been cleaned out, they say. We haven't had a pouch through from San Francisco since the one that left there the eighteenth of May."

"Can't they drive the Indians off?"

"Can when they get men enough, I reckon. But they had bad luck when they went out to Pyramid Lake to drive 'em. Major Ormsby took out about a hundred men. The Indians ambushed them, and there wasn't half the outfit got back alive."

"How is it through Nebraska? Any trouble?"

"Not a bit so far, with the Indians. Everything quiet. . . . Let's go back and see if Tipton is all right, then I reckon I'd better go and get some supper."

To the steady beat of sixteen hoofs, and the chucking of hubs on axles, the stagecoach bowled along. Jeff, on the box beside the driver, spoke after a long silence. "Looks to me," he ventured, "from what I've seen of the country so far, that riding the Pony Express wouldn't be so hard— I mean, of course, if a fellow didn't get held up by robbers. There's a good road that a fellow couldn't hardly miss if he tried. These 'home' stations set out mighty good meals, and there's plenty of these little 'swing' stations, as they call 'em, in between, where a fellow changes horses. Looks easy to me."

The driver chuckled. "You're seeing the smooth part of the layout, son, along here between St. Joe and Fort Kearny. There's been enough travel over this here trail to make a regular road out of it. Most o' the emigrant outfits from Missouri go this way. Russell, Majors, and Waddell have been using this trail for years for their heavy freighting, and

42

they've got their stations purty well fixed up. Then the stage business makes a difference, too. Things ain't so handy when you get out West."

"What kind of a place is Julesburg?" Jeff asked.

"Toughest town between St. Joe and Salt Lake City, Julesburg is," declared the driver, with relish. "Regular hangout for gamblers and worse. Guess there ain't quite so many hoss thieves round there now, though, since Jack Slade is superintendent. You didn't hear anything about who it might of been that waylaid your brother, did you?"

"No, sir, I don't know a thing about it, except that they tried to hold up the Pony Express, and that he brought the mail in, but they shot him."

"Slade has cleaned out quite a few of them holdup gangs," commented the driver. "But there's some yet, of course. They say Pete Anderson's the worst rustler out in that country. That is, unless Slade has rounded him up lately. But if he has, I hain't heard about it."

"Do you know Mr. Slade?"

"Well, I never seen him, that I know of," returned the driver. "But I've heard lots about him." He gave Jeff a keen, sidewise glance; seemed about to say something more, then checked himself.

"Is Julesburg a big place?" Jeff asked, after a moment's silence.

"Naw! Four or five buildings and a few dugouts. Wood's so scarce out there they haul most o' what they use clean through from Cottonwood Springs, better'n a hundred miles. The fellers that ride out o' Julesburg don't see much o' the butter and eggs and cream in the coffee and fresh lettuce and radishes and pieplant pie that they set out for 'em back here along the Little Blue!"

Jeff, thinking of his brother, said nothing. For a little time the rumble of the coach, the beating hoofs, the murmur of voices inside the stage were the only sounds.

"Ha! There she blows!" The driver gestured westward with his whip. Jeff, looking keenly, sighted a tiny blob of color on the horizon.

"What is it?"

"Flag at Fort Kearny. That's quite a place. I'm always sorta glad to get in there, seems like there's something solid about the whole layout. It's the main place between the Missouri River and the mountains. The freight outfits and emigrant wagons from Omaha, Nebraska City, Plattsmouth, and St. Joe all go through there."

The stage rolled on. The flag on its tall staff showed more plainly. Soon the numerous buildings of the fort came into view, grouped on the south side of the trail.

"There's the post stables," said the driver, pointing with his whip. "That there row of buildings this side the parade ground is the soldiers' quarters. The officers' quarters is just across the parade ground. Yonder's the stage station. You're two hundred and seventy-three miles out o' St. Joe when you get here."

The office, eating house, and stable of the Central Overland, California and Pike's Peak Express Company stood on the right-hand side of the trail, a few hundred yards west of the fort. The driver drew up his four-horse team with a flourish in front of the office, tossed the reins to hostlers who

44

ran forward, and descended from his box. Jeff jumped down after him. The stage passengers climbed stiffly out, brushed off some of the dust that covered their clothing, and went in for supper. Jeff paid twenty-five cents for a doughnut and a cup of muddy coffee, and scrambled back to his seat on the box before anyone had time to preempt it, and before the new driver appeared.

Perched on the high seat, he looked about while he waited. There was, as the driver had remarked, something solid in the appearance of Fort Kearny, with its neatly painted frame buildings and its rows of shade trees flanking the parade ground. The fort and the stage buildings stood on slightly elevated ground; one could see far east and west along the level valley of the Platte River. A low line of bluffs, two miles away at the nearest point, followed the south edge of the valley. On the north the view was partly cut off by the cottonwoods and willows which skirted the river and covered the islands.

Jeff yawned and stretched. Two hundred and seventy-three miles of day and night riding had tired him out, keyed up though he was with anxiety about Chet. But he had learned something. The best place to sleep on a stagecoach was not inside, jammed upright on a crowded seat, but down in the front boot, under the box. If there happened to be several sacks of fairly soft mail down there, and not too much baggage, a chap could curl up and get some real rest while the outfit, changing teams now and then, bowled on through the night.

Darkness closed in about the time the stage pulled out of Plum Creek. Jeff slid into the boot, and slept through

45

Willow Island, Midway, and Gilman's Station. Breakfast-time came at Cottonwood Springs.

Then a long day. The stagecoach wheels rasped and chucked along the rutted trail, or ground with oddly muffled sound through long stretches of sand. The Platte, almost as muddy as the Missouri, ran ever eastward in its wide, sandy bed, while the trail followed the south bank up the steadily rising valley. Sometimes a rocky bluff crowded the trail over almost to the river's cut bank; sometimes the bottom widened out in broad spaces.

Jeff watched the country with interested eyes. "What made that?" he asked the driver, pointing to a deep-worn, dusty path about a foot wide, running from the river's edge back across the bottom.

"Buffalo. Come down to drink. Always use the same track."

V   CAPTAIN SLADE

Dusk of the long summer day, and darkness, and at last the stage pulled into Julesburg. Jeff got down stiff and sore from the high seat. He stood for a moment or two, his little bundle of clothing and his blanket under his arm, watching the change of teams and drivers in the flickering light of a pair of oil lanterns, looking up and down the town's single row of low buildings. The solid ground seemed moving under his feet after the four days' lurch and sway of the stage. Foreboding touched him; he dreaded to seek that for which he had come.

Then he spoke to a hostler who was taking away the jaded teams just unhitched from the stage: "Where's that Express rider that got shot the other day?"

"They've got him in the back end of Hogan's," the man replied, scanning Jeff in the lantern light.

"Where's Hogan's?"

"Third place down the line from the station."

Jeff walked into the small, cluttered store. "How is he—Chet—the rider?" he asked, fearfully, of the man behind the counter. "I'm his brother."

"He's been purty bad, sort of feverish." He glanced toward a closed door in the rear. "But he's asleep now. I wouldn't bother him. Sleep'll do him more good than anything else. Wait till he wakes up."

Jeff drew a long breath. He stood silent, his eyes turned toward the closed door, then tiptoed out of the place. Hope awoke in his heart. His spirits rose. As he stood outside in the short, dark street, he realized all at once that he was very hungry.

The stage had rolled away in the darkness on the trail to Denver. The eating house was empty, save for the frowzy youth who was cook, waiter, and cashier all in one. He stirred himself at Jeff's request, slid bacon, fried potatoes, hard bread, and coffee across the counter, and took seventy-five cents in payment.

Jeff ate everything. He was still hungry when he finished, but restrained his impulse to order something more. After waiting what seemed a decent interval, he went again to the store where his brother was.

"Is he still asleep?" he asked the storekeeper.

"I wuz just going to look."

Jeff walked with light tread behind the man, who took a kerosene lamp from its swinging bracket on the wall and opened the door in the rear.

The lamp's yellow gleam lit a small room, a rough plank bunk, a shadowy, blanketed figure. The sound of hard

48

breathing came to the pair in the doorway. The man backed out, taking Jeff with him.

"Still asleep. We'll let him rest. That's Slade's orders. Said this morning he'd send him East on the next stage, if he seemed strong enough t' stand it. Wants to git him somewhere so's they can git the bullet out."

"Who is Slade, a doctor?"

"Naw, ain't you never heard of *him*? Superintendent of the stage and Pony Express from here to Rocky Ridge. No, he ain't no doctor, but he's seen plenty of hombres with bullet holes through 'em. No doctors in this country." He set the lamp back in its bracket.

"Where was Chet hit?"

"In the chest, kinda to one side. . . . You better go turn in, son, and drop back in here in the morning to see your brother. I sleep on a cot here in the store. I'll look after him if he needs anything in the night."

Jeff tiptoed out, his mind awhirl with dread and elation. Chet badly hurt, a bullet in his body, but getting better!

He walked restlessly up and down the short street. A single light showed at the stage station. Two or three buildings were dark. The yellow radiance of kerosene lamps flared through the windows of one of the false-fronted structures. Jeff stepped up to the open door and looked in.

The room was low and long, the cedar logs of its walls showing dim and dark under the flickering lamps. Four men were playing cards at a table. A bartender was lounging behind the bar which lined one side of the place.

Jeff had no desire to go in. He was turning away when heavy footfalls sounded on the low platform where he stood, and a man walked past him into the saloon. Jeff paused, then, watching.

The man who strode in was about five feet eight inches in height, well-set and muscular, with an erect carriage that hinted of military training. The trousers of his neat blue suit were tucked inside his boots. Jeff caught hardly more than a glimpse of his face, shaded from the uncertain light by a broad-brimmed hat.

Play stopped at the table. The bartender came alert. "Good evening, Captain," he greeted, carefully.

"Good evening, everyone!" The phrase was somehow menacing.

The newcomer walked up to the bar, while his hard glance roved the room. "Gentlemen, I invite you all to join me in a drink," he announced.

The four players scrambled to their feet, one of them upsetting a chair, and lined up at the bar.

The bartender slid out a row of glasses and filled them from a tall bottle. All waited till the host raised his glass; the round was drunk in silence.

"Have another," the host invited, in slightly more genial manner.

Politely, cautiously, the four begged to be excused. It appeared none of them was in the best of health. When the host's silence seemed to give consent, they sidled away, after a watchful pause, and drifted back to their table. They fingered their cards, but did not resume play.

Left to himself, the man in front of the bar filled his own glass, and drank leisurely. He was setting down the empty glass when another man walked through the doorway. The dust of the trail was on this latest comer, he looked like what he was, a freighter. He stood still, blinking under the lamps, not prepared for but instantly rallying to the quick invitation: "Come here, friend, and join me in a drink."

"Don't keer ef I do. I been whacking mules all th' way from O'Fallon's Bluffs, and—" He walked up to the bar.

The bartender filled two glasses.

The air was tense. Jeff, against his will, drew a step closer, watching. He saw the formidable host lift a glass with his left hand. The freighter grasped his draft; in the same instant the other's free hand flicked over it in a deft movement almost imperceptible. A something showed now in the freighter's glass. It might have been, in size and shape, the half of a dried peach.

The freighter stared, he hesitated.

"Drink!" commanded the host.

As the freighter still delayed, the other's right hand flashed to his belt with a motion the eye could hardly follow, and the flickering oil lamps shone on a heavy Colt's revolver covering the hesitating guest. The host rapped the bar sharply with his left hand. His voice was imperious. "Drink!"

Breathing stopped for an instant. Then the freighter took up his glass. He drank, with wry face. He left about a third of his liquor. He rubbed his mouth with the back of his hand, then fished something out of his glass and laid it gingerly on the bar. A faint sound, like breath released, sounded in the narrow room. The host stuck the Colt back into its holster.

Jeff, ill at ease, backed off, and stole away from the lamplight into the unlighted street. He had no more than reached sheltering darkness when two of the players walked out, with cautious backward glances. "I ain't got any more business in there, right now," one said, low-voiced, as they passed Jeff.

"Me neither," agreed the other. "The Captain's okay, so far. I don't mind seein' him have his little joke, specially on a stranger. But he's workin' himself up. I know the signs. He's liable to git ugly purty soon. I seen him onct at Cottonwood—" They passed beyond earshot.

Jeff did not understand. But he knew he had no business in that place. He wished he had someone with whom he could talk. He took a few turns up and down the short, dark street. The night was clear and only pleasantly cool. He made up his mind, with his fingers touching the worn buckskin pouch that held his scanty cash, there was no use paying a dollar for a bunk in the station house. He went in and got his blanket from the corner where he had left it, and lay down on the sandy ground beside a building next to the stage station.

He was tired, he slept a while dreamlessly. Past midnight he roused, not knowing at first where he was, then quickly coming alert.

A lantern hanging on the side of the station cast a yellow aureole, outlining horses and men. Two horses, three men, he saw, as sleep cleared from his eyes. One horse panting, spattered with foam, wet from fording the Platte River crossing, the other horse fresh, anxious, tugging at the bit.

The men moved fast. They jerked a mochila from one

saddle and flung it onto the other; the fresh rider swung into the leather. A quick tattoo of hoofs and the eastbound Pony Express was out of Julesburg.

The stationman hooked the lantern over his arm and led the other horse back to the stables, the tired rider clumped into the station, the receding hoofbeats grew faint and died away. But Jeff thrilled as he lay there in the darkness, for all that the Pony Express had ever meant to him of romance and gallant adventure came pulsing back. His first purpose, lately driven aside by concern for Chet, came to the fore and turned into hard resolve. He was bound now to get on as rider. He shifted and turned a long while before he again slept.

The sun in his eyes woke him. He got to his feet, brushing the sand out of his clothes, and looked curiously around over the "toughest town between St. Joe and Salt Lake City."

The raw light of early morning was on the unkempt little place. No trees broke the sun's glare. No painted houses, no neat fences, as at Fort Kearny. A cedar-log stage station and eating house, a long, log stable, a blacksmith shop, two or three false-fronted frame buildings ranged in a row alongside the trail, a few scattering sod houses. Julesburg was dreary, sun-blasted, forbidding.

He went first to the store building where Chet was. The door was locked, so he went to the eating house and got breakfast, then came back. This time the storekeeper was up and stirring. Jeff followed him to Chet's bunk.

"Chet! How you making it?"

"First rate."

"Does—does it hurt you much, where you got hit?"

"Not so bad, now. I'll be all right, Jeff. In a few days."

Jeff, ever sensitive, his feeling now wrought high and keen, knew that they two, always so close to each other, were playing a part as they talked. He must not show the shock he felt at the sight of Chet's pale, drawn face, the fear that ran through him. And Chet, for his sake, was making light of his wound.

"Who was it shot you?"

"Don't know. Dark. Two fellows. Got a glimpse of 'em —storming, lightning. Think probably 'twas Pete Anderson. He's head of a gang—been making trouble." Chet paused. It was, Jeff saw, hard for him to talk.

Silence, while hot anger mounted in Jeff's heart, mounted and formed into set purpose. Two things now to do. Get on the Pony Express, and then—

"What does this Pete Anderson look like, Chet?"

"Slim, kinda tall. Sort of sharp-faced. Dark-haired, they say."

"Say, Chet, you—you better go back East, where you can have a doctor to—to look at you. I'll go along and take care of you. What say?"

"I reckon I'll have to. No need your going. You see Slade. He may need a good rider. Get on if you can. It's the real stuff, Jeff. I'll be back—in a few weeks. Then we'll both be on."

"Well—if you say so, Chet. Slade, he's superintendent, is he?"

"Yeah. And say—"

54

"What?"

"When you go to see him, call him *Captain* Slade. He likes to have 'em call him Captain."

"Was he in the army?"

"Can't prove it by me. I heard 'em say he was in the Mexican War." [1] *

Silence again, while Jeff's glance roved from Chet's face to the bare walls, and back.

"Reckon I better be going, Chet. I'll come and see you some more, after a while."

"All right. So long."

The glare of the afternoon sun outlined Jeff's shadow as he stepped into the doorway of the eating house, coming from a watch at Chet's bunkside.

"Guess you can see Slade now, if you want to," the youthful cook said, without waiting to be asked. "He's in the office."

Jeff walked carefully into an adjoining room, not sure how he would be met. The man who glanced up at him from the desk behind the railing was the man he had watched at the bar the night before. He wore the same well-cut blue suit. His brown hair, under the light from the small window, glinted with copper tints. His muscular neck, his powerful shoulders, the color in his face laid by sun and wind hinted that he had not spent much of his life behind a desk. The blue-gray eyes that swung on Jeff were direct and not unfriendly. Yet as he met their gaze Jeff felt, like chill air flowing, a personality implacable and hard. [2]

* Notes begin on page 195.

"Are you Mr. Slade, sir?" he asked, hastily.

"Captain Slade, lad, if you please. What is it?"

"Beg your pardon, Captain." Jeff reddened in confusion as it came to him that he had forgotten what Chet had told him. "I—I'm Chet Harlowe's brother, sir. I came out here from St. Joe to see about him. And I thought—can you use another rider on the Express, Captain?"

Slade's eyes measured him. "Have you ridden much?" he asked, pleasantly.

"Yes, sir. Ever since I can remember. I was out with Bill Sanderson after wild horses this spring."

"With Sanderson, eh? If you trailed with him, you can ride. Yes, I can use a fellow of the right sort. Can you go on right away?"

"Yes, sir, only—I thought maybe I ought to go back East with my brother, when he goes. But he says—"

"You couldn't do your brother any good. Take a surgeon for that. If you want on today, I can use you. Two of my riders quit."

"All right, sir, I'm ready."

Slade got up. Shifting his gun belt, he hunted through a drawer that held a revolver, boxes of cartridges, a pair of spurs. "Here," he said, as he found a slip of paper. "This is the Pony Express rider's oath. Hold up your hand and repeat this after me."

It was strangely unlike that time Jeff had listened to Chet repeating, phrase by phrase, the oath before Alexander Majors. Slade rattled the words off, scarcely looking at the printed slip before him. Jeff, repeating, felt no thrill. It all seemed casual; he went on, his voice low and steady, to the last . . . "all my acts as to win the confidence of my employers. So help me God."

"Sign it," Slade directed. He had found a pen, a little wooden-jacketed bottle of ink, in the tumbled litter of the drawer.

Jeff signed. Now, as his hand formed the letters, there was that which was like the day he had watched Chet in Majors' office. Once more a prevision of danger came uncannily to him.

"I'll send you up to Mud Springs," Slade said. "You'll likely have a regular run out of there. Do you know the trail?"

"No, sir, I don't, but I reckon I can find the way."

"A teamster will be going up the line tomorrow morning with supplies. You can ride up with him."

Slade, with this, would have turned to other matters. But Jeff spoke:

"Who do you suppose it was shot Chet, sir?"

"Don't know. Might have been Pete Anderson."

"What does this Anderson look like, Captain? I'm going to look for him, and if I find him I'll—"

Jeff drew back, startled into silence. Deadly anger flared in Slade's face. His blue-gray eyes, to Jeff's astounded gaze, turned almost black. His voice came cruel and hard.

"Your job is to carry the mail. You do that, and leave outlaw-hunting to me. I'll attend to Anderson, in the way I've attended to others. Understand?"

"Yes, sir."

"I think your brother can go East on the next stage." Slade's manner was suddenly almost genial. "He'll be all

57

right when they get him patched up. I'll have a place for him when he gets well, if he wants it. He's a good rider. See that you do as well, Jeff."

"I'll do my best, Captain."

"This Thirty-mile Ridge is a dry stretch." The buck-board driver pointed with his whip to a mound of gravel and yellow clay, half hidden by wild sunflowers. It hardly needed his light pull on the reins to bring the team to a standstill. "See that pile o' dirt?"

"Yes," Jeff replied, alertly. "What is it?"

"Place where they tried to find water. Went down more'n a hundred feet—all they got was a dry hole. They ain't no water, 'cept a little in the buffalo wallows after a wet spell, from Pole Creek station to Mud Springs."

"How far is that?"

"Twenty-eight miles."

"Long ways for a horse in hot weather."

"Yeh, but they kinda get used to it."

The driver shifted in his seat under the blasting July sun. The mouse-colored mustangs stood in their tracks, the sweat quickly beginning to dry on them in the oven-like air. The buffalo grass, brown, crisp, undulated to empty horizons.

"Giddap!" shouted the driver. The wiry team went into its steady trot. The empty prairie, looking all alike to Jeff, slipped past for another hour. The land then became rougher, brown hillocks rising and falling like waves in a choppy sea. "Kinda bad country right in here," the driver remarked.

"Bad?"

58

"Yep, fellow can't see no distance—gives Indians too good a chance to sneak up on you."

Presently they topped a long rise. The driver pointed with his whip. "There she is."

A MILE to northward, two dark square dots showed—the Mud Springs station and stable.

The station house was a cedar-log shanty about twelve feet square. Its low ridge pole, running from gable to gable, held up other close-laid poles, overlaid with a thick layer of hay and a top covering of sod. Blobs of resin hung sticky on the logs of the south side, under the drawing sun.

A young fellow stood in the doorway watching. He walked lightly across the hard-trodden ground in front of the cabin as the driver dropped his reins. "Hello, Hardtack!" he called, grinning.

"Hi, there, Handsome," returned the driver. "Brung you a rider."

Jeff swung down and the station keeper faced him.

About Jeff's height, two or three years older, fifteen pounds heavier, he looked ready for anything. His leather-dark face lit with a smile; he held out a hard hand. "Lacy's the name," he said. "Jack, for short. What's yours?"

That first contact, that good-natured, reckless glance of brown, bright eyes, woke Jeff's liking.

"Harlowe," he said. "Jeff Harlowe. Everybody calls me Jeff."

"Related to Chet Harlowe? How's he getting along, anyway?"

"Brother. He's some better. They started him East on the stage this morning. Want to get him to a hospital."

"Been riding down on the East End, have you?"

"No, I'm just starting in."

"Well, it isn't so bad out here," Lacy said, "that is, if we can keep from starving to death." He gave Jeff a wink. "What've you got for us this time?" he went on, turning to the driver, still on the buckboard seat. "I suppose you fetched that roll of country butter and the eggs I sent for?"

The driver's glance roved over the stuff in the buckboard. "Well, I'll be jiggered!" he exclaimed. "They must've fell out back yonder, when we run over a rock. Mighty sorry, Jack, but they're gone."

It was one of their standing jokes. Butter and eggs were not to be had along that part of the Pony Express trail.

"Anyhow, here's some stuff that'll stick to your ribs," said the driver. "Beans, bacon, hardtack, coffee, 'n sugar. Here's half a bushel o' spuds, too. And the hoss feed."

He was stirring himself as he talked. Lacy and Jeff helped unload the boxes, and half a dozen sacks of oats. The driver led his team over to the spring, in a draw north of the station, and watered them. Then he drove on north, with a farewell wave of his hand. He had told Jeff he was figuring on making the next relay station that evening.

"Well, what do you think of the layout?" asked Lacy, as the two reentered the station.

Jeff looked around the single room. A small sheet-iron stove stood almost in the center, two built-in bunks lined the west wall, a rough plank table stood under the one small window. Overhead, wisps of hay showed between the roof-poles. The smooth, hard-packed dirt floor had been neatly swept.

"Looks all right to me."

"It's nothing to brag on, but I reckon it could be worse."

"You been here quite a while, Jack?"

"Ever since the Express started. Little over three months, now."

Jeff looked out through the doorway. Beyond the bare, hoof-marked space in front of the station ran the trail, deep-rutted but grass-grown. "Is there much travel through here?" he asked.

"Not so much, anymore. Used to be a lively old trail, they tell me, when the California gold rush was on. Now they're mostly heading for the Colorado diggings. Nearly everybody from the East switches off at Julesburg and goes south."

"Is there a stage through here?"

"Yeah, twice a month. Used to be weekly. That was

when Hockaday and Chorpenning were carrying the mail. Hockaday had the contract as far as Salt Lake City and Chorpenning had it from there on. But the Post Office Department cut that out. It sure ruined those fellows."

Lacy glanced at the westering sun. "Time to feed," he remarked. "Come on and look the stock over."

Jeff stood outside the low log stable and watched. Lacy led out a pony. "Here's Bonny," he announced.

Bonny was a bright bay. His head was lean and well chiseled, he carried his ears forward. He walked with quick, smooth action. Jeff noted that his hind feet set down well ahead of the track of the front ones, as Lacy led him over to the spring and back.

Next came a coarser, heavier dun-colored pony, deep-bodied, short-legged. "This is Tipton," Lacy said, as he led him past.

"Now Mack, and that's all, except the mules."

The black pony pranced, danced, pirouetted. He was taller, more rangy than the others, his glossy coat, his hard, clean legs showed quality. His ears were back. When he settled down to a walk he stepped out quickly, smoothly.

"Which one will you take?" Lacy asked, as he went along the manger row, dumping a small pailful of oats into each feed box.

"The bay looks good, for an all-around horse," Jeff said, judicially. "But if I was trying to make a getaway—if somebody was after me—I believe I'd rather be on the black."

Lacy gave him a quick glance. "I reckon you know horses."

"I don't claim to know so much about them, but I've rid-

63

den ever since I can remember. . . . These mules are for the stage, I reckon?"

"Yeah. Eating their blamed heads off, but the company has to have a couple of fresh span here ready when the stage does take a notion to come along."

Supper over, the boys squatted on their heels in front of the station, leaning back against the log wall, while the sun went down and coolness crept into the air.

"What about a gun when I'm riding?" Jeff asked. "All the riders out here carry something, don't they? I didn't ask about that down at Julesburg."

"Yes. There's two revolvers in there. One for the rider." He brought out a muzzle-loading, cap-and-ball forty-four Colt.

Jeff took it, hefted it, leveled it steadily at a stunted sunflower beside the trail. "Say, Jack, what sort of looking fellow is this Pete Anderson?"

Lacy glanced curiously at him. "He's tall and slim, I never saw him—that is close, so's to get a look at his face. I don't know as there's anything special about his looks, only he's got a little whitish scar, up sort of high on his temple, where a bullet nicked him. Fellow that used to run around with him, before Pete went bad, told me about that. Why?"

Jeff turned the Colt over in his hand thoughtfully, then handed it back. "Oh, I just thought I'd like to know him, if I ever run onto him. . . . Feels like a real gun," he said, making his voice sound indifferent.

"Good as they make, I reckon. You probably won't need it, but it don't hurt to have one."

"Sure don't."

64

The sunlight of midafternoon was baking the heat-blasted plains. Within the sweep of the horizon the only shade was a narrow belt on the east side of the cedar-pole, sod-roof station and stable at Mud Springs. Jeff and Lacy stood in the sheltered space beside the station. They peered south.

"About time for him to be a-showing." Lacy glanced a second time at his heavy silver watch before shoving it back into his trousers pocket.

"You say he's usually about on time?"

"Fairly near it, most generally. Look, there he comes!"

A mile away, a horse and rider topped a ridge and sped toward them. Only for a little time they showed, then dipped behind a swell of the choppy prairie.

Lacy hurried back to the stable. He led Bonny, the bay, already saddled and bridled, from its dusky interior.

Jeff stood where he was, hitching the holster that held his Colt's revolver. In buckskin jacket and fringed buckskin trousers he looked trim and fit; his broad-brimmed felt hat shaded a sunburned, eager face.

The incoming rider showed now, nearer. A far-off "eeh-yah!" sounded on the shimmering air. The faint tattoo of hoofs grew louder.

Another moment and the horseman reined up his foam-spattered pony in front of the station door. It stood in its tracks, with head drooping. Twenty-eight miles from Pole Creek station, without water.

"Hi, Bill," Lacy greeted.

The rider swung lightly from his seat, and in the same motion pulled the mochila from his saddle. "Purty good bunch o' mail today," he grinned. "Sixteen pounds."

Jeff grabbed the mochila. Lacy caught one end and helped fit it down over the bay's saddle. "Steady, now, boy, don't get excited," he counseled. He might have been speaking to the pony, or to Jeff. Each was nervously anxious to be off.

"See any Indians this time?" Lacy asked.

"Half a dozen or so—looked like a hunting party. Saw a fair-sized herd o' buffalo along Lodge Pole Creek, five hundred head or better. Man, it sure is hot!" He jerked off his hat and ran his fingers through a shock of yellow hair.

The fresh pony snorted and thrust at the bit. Lacy held it firmly. Jeff rolled his slicker coat and with feverish haste strapped it across the mochila, behind the cantle.

"All set?" Lacy asked.

"Yup, let 'er go!" Jeff caught his stirrup, swung up, and settled firmly into the saddle as the released pony made its first bound. Its hoofs spattered dust and gravel over the two left at the station.

Lacy pulled his watch, pocketed it again. "Minute 'n a half. The kid's sure anxious to make good." He set down the time of the mail's arrival and departure in his record book.

Jeff held his pony in for the first mile, slowing it at times to a jog trot. When it was well warmed up he shook it out into a long, steady gallop.

The sun beat down blastingly. The air that fanned his cheeks was as dry as that out of an oven's mouth. With every "klop-klop" of the pony's hoofs a burst of white alkali dust rose behind.

66

For nearly twelve miles the trail ran due north from Mud Springs. Then it dipped over the bluffs into the North Platte bottom, and turned northwestward up the valley.

Now on Jeff's right was the Platte, shimmering in its wide sandy bed, fringed with cottonwood and stunted willows. The bluffs beyond the river and the closer line of hills on his left were brown with buffalo grass, garnished with sage-brush and now and then a plum thicket in the mouth of a coulee. Ahead, slowing rising as he neared, was the tall shaft of Chimney Rock.

On! On! His pony, wet with sweat and foam, turned from bay to dirty cream as alkali dust settled and caked upon it. But it held its steady gallop. The relay station, low, brown-baked, showed in the westering sunlight.

"Eeh-yah!" Jeff yelled. No sign of life. He yelled again. A man ran out and darted into the stable. When Jeff swung down, the fresh pony, a slim, white-stockinged black, was ready for him.

"How're you making it?" asked the stationman.

"All right." Jeff spoke through cracked lips. He and the man jerked the mochila off and flung it across the fresh pony's saddle. Jeff restrapped his slicker. He gulped a drink of brackish water. Then he stepped into the leather and the black pony darted away with him.

"Minute, flat," the stationman remarked to himself, as he waved farewell. He entered the time in his book.

Steadily, like one who knew nothing else, Jeff rode. He nursed the black along skillfully. He was at home in the saddle; but he now began to feel the strain of riding the Pony Express.

67

"These ponies all know the trail," Lacy had assured him. "You don't need to worry because you ain't never been over the line before. Just give 'em their head, they'll take you through."

The blasting sun swung slowly lower as horse and rider kept their westward way. Its rays hit them fair in the face for a last long hour, then it dipped behind a distant butte. Scott's Bluff, cedar-fringed, stood out clear in the evening glow. Laramie Peak, a far, bluish cone, rose small against the westward horizon. Coolness crept into the air.

A pelican rose from a buffalo wallow beside the trail at the sound of the flying pony's hoofs and flapped away on heavy wings. A coyote watched the rider from a bluff. Jeff passed a group of emigrants encamped for night, their wagons drawn up in a circle against Indian attack. Their campfire gleamed in the dusk; hands waved, voices shouted a greeting as he galloped past.

Then darkness settled down upon the trail, the chill darkness of the high plains and foothills. Jeff unstrapped his slicker and drew it on. The pony knew the trail, as Lacy had told him; he let it have its head. So he came to another station where a station keeper awaited his coming. He made another quick change of ponies under the starlight, and was away on the last lap of his ride.

A pain gripped his side. He was deadly tired from the jolt and pound of the saddle. But the night air now bore the scent of sagebrush and cedar, and a hint of dampness from the swiftly flowing Platte and Laramie.

Under the starlight, at last, dim outlines of a stockade and buildings showed. Jeff heard water rippling. His pony's

68

hoofs grated in a bank of gravel. It hesitated an instant, then plunged into the Laramie River ford. A splashing, a grinding of steel-shod hoofs on rock, and the pony scrambled up the further bank. It shook itself, picked up its gallop, and soon swung up in front of the Express station.

Jeff got down stiffly. His head felt too light. He jerked the mochila off and handed it over to the waiting rider, a slim young fellow whose smiling face showed brown as an Indian's in the light of the stationman's lantern. There was a word or two about the mail and the trail. Then the youth galloped westward into the darkness, heading for the upper reaches of the Platte and the high mountain country on his fresh and eager pony.

Jeff gave his spent pony to the stationman, who led it off to a stable. He then sat down on the ground in the darkness, his back to the log wall of the station. Just to sit there quietly was luxury unspeakable.

The man came back from the stable, his lantern making a yellow blob in the black night. He came close to Jeff. "Want some grub?"

"No, I'm not hungry. I'd like a good drink, though."

"Come on in."

Jeff forced himself up and followed his host into the low-roofed station. The lantern's half-light showed a rough plank table, a sheet-iron camp stove, shelves with dishes and provisions, and two bunks, one above the other.

The man reached and brought something down from the top shelf. "Here," he invited, turning to the table. "Have one on the house." He set a nearly full bottle of whisky and a small glass before Jeff.

69

"No, I didn't mean that, mister. I don't drink. All I want is some water."

"Pard, this here water ain't fit to drink. Sometimes I get some from the river, that's all right, but all I got tonight is outa the well. 'Tain't good. Have a nip outa the bottle. It'll brace you up."

"No, thanks just the same. Let me try the water."

"Yonder's the bucket. Help yourself."

Jeff took a mouthful. He could not swallow more.

He glanced out of the doorway into the darkness, half minded to find his way down to the river, then turned back. He looked around the narrow room. "I reckon I'll turn in," he said, then. "What bunk shall I take?"

"The riders take that there top one."

Jeff climbed into the upper bunk. Its spring was a criss-cross of rawhide strips, its mattress a folded blanket. He pillowed his head on his slicker, drew a blanket around him, and slept. He dreamed again and again of a cool, sweet spring he had known in Missouri, but whenever he tried to dip up a gourdful of the water it drew back just out of his reach.

He roused to a clatter and rattle. A sharp-cut square of sunlight etched the uneven log wall opposite the open door. The sheet-iron stove was aglow with a fire of cedar chunks. The bearded stationman hovered over it. Aroma drifted from a blubbering coffee pot. Bacon sizzled in a pan; potatoes snapped and hissed in a skillet.

"Better roll out o' there, young fellow," advised the man. "I'll have the grub pile stacked right soon now." Jeff scrambled down.

70

Hardtack, bacon, fried potatoes, coffee. That was the bill of fare for breakfast. For dinner and supper it would be the same, with beans perhaps added. The stage driver on the stretch east of Fort Kearny had been right—the milk, butter, eggs, fresh vegetables, and soft bread of the stage stations in eastern Kansas and Nebraska were unknown along the Pony Express trail in the sagebrush country. Jeff ate with appetite, drank two big cups of black coffee, and felt ready for anything.

"What time does the eastbound mail usually get here?" he asked.

"She's due tomorrow around the middle of the forenoon. You can't tell for sure till you see him coming. It's a long old run from Sacramento. They haven't hardly got straightened out yet west of Salt Lake after that Indian trouble. And sometimes a sandstorm on the desert holds the boys up. You'll have plenty time to look around here."

Jeff found Fort Laramie more impressive even than Fort Kearny. There were more buildings, though they were unpainted. The two-storied headquarters house, with its double-decked porch with seven pillars, was the largest building he had seen west of St. Joseph. Beyond the fort the foothills rose to the great bulk of Laramie Peak.

The hours went quickly, yet he was glad when the eastbound Express rider showed up, almost on time. The mail was light. Jeff was ready, and got off without losing a minute.

The hundred-mile ride to Mud Springs was just a ride. The trail seemed shorter going back. A fresh pony stood waiting for him at each relay station. The weather had

71

turned cooler, it was easier to make good time. The long, bright summer day was closing when he topped the last rise and saw, half a mile to southward, the weathered Mud Springs station. He raised the usual warning yell as he galloped closer. There was Jack Lacy, holding a saddled pony. An instant later Bill Johnson walked around the corner of the building.

"How'd you make it, old-timer?" Lacy asked.

"All right."

Bill Johnson's only greeting was a grin, wide and friendly.

"You're half an hour ahead of time, but a little thing like that won't make Bill sore," Lacy chaffed. "Gives him a chance to loaf some going down."

"Sure," grinned Bill.

They jerked the mochila off one saddle and slapped it onto the other as they talked. Bill caught his stirrup, waved his hand, and was off for Julesburg.

Lacy led the other pony to the stable. Jeff walked back and forth in front of the station, limbering his cramped muscles. He paused as Lacy came back. It was as good a time as any to talk.

"Say, Jack?"

"What?"

"What kind of a fellow is Captain Slade, anyhow?"

Lacy glanced at him. "How do you mean?"

"Well, I saw something queer that night I laid over in Julesburg, and I didn't know——"

"What'd you see?"

Jeff told about the freighter.

Lacy listened closely. "So the fellow fished it out o' the

glass and laid it down on the bar, did he?" he exclaimed, when Jeff paused. "Wish I'd been there—I always wanted to see the Captain pull that trick once!"

"*But what was it?* What'd he drop in the glass?"

"Don't you know about *that?* But no—I reckon you might not have heard about it, either. You just got out here."

Jeff waited, but Lacy remained provokingly silent.

"What was it, anyhow, Jack?"

"*Jules Reni's ear!*"

"Ear! What'd you mean, ear?"

Lacy smiled in superior fashion. "I suppose you never heard of old Jules Reni, did you?"

"Don't know as I ever did."

"Well, he was the first fellow that ever set stakes down there where that town is now. They used to call the place Jules' Ranch. But after the town started they got to calling it Julesburg.

"Old Jules was a tough hombre, they say. Big and mean and a regular whisky soak. Plenty notches on his gun. The stage company hired him for agent down there.

"Somehow or other, the stage company got to losing a lot of horses. They sort of faded away overnight along at the relay stations.

"A man by the name of Williams was general superintendent for the stage company then. He was a nice chap, they say, only he didn't understand conditions out on the plains very well. After a while the company let him go and put Ben Ficklin in his place."

"I know Mister Ficklin," Jeff remarked.

73

"Well, Ficklin knows the stage business. He mighty soon made some changes along the line. Julesburg was the worst place of all. He put Jack Slade in there as division agent or superintendent, and told him to straighten things out.

"Slade came out and started looking around. He soon found out old Jules was in with the outfit that was stealing the company's horses. Slade rounded up most of the stock and got it back, and of course he discharged Jules.

"So Jules laid for him with a shotgun loaded with buckshot. He nailed him, and almost finished him up right there. Slade was in a hospital back East for quite a while. When he got patched up, he came back West. He went to the commandant at Fort Laramie and told him just what the layout was. The only way to straighten things out, he figured, was to get rid of Jules. The commandant told him to go ahead.

"Jules always had some fellows with him. Slade got two or three good men of his own and trailed the outfit. They got Jules. Slade tied him up to a post in a corral and gradually filled him full of lead. Then he cut off his ears. He nailed one of 'em onto the corral fence, and carried the other one around with him. 'Course it all sort of shriveled up— I heard a fellow say it looked something like a dried peach.

"Once in a while when Slade goes into a barroom and they don't wait on him quite quick enough he'll reach in his vest pocket and take out that dried ear and throw it on the bar. 'Change *that*, will you!' he'll say. Then the bartender will just about fall over himself hustling around to give him whatever he wants. Then sometimes, usually when he already has a few drinks under his belt, he'll invite some fellow to have one with him, and then, just as the chap goes to raise his glass, Slade'll drop that ear in it, then make him go ahead and drink. That's what you saw." [3]

Jeff's startled gray eyes were intent on his companion's face. He saw that Lacy was telling the truth. A shiver ran through him; he shifted uneasily. "Why," he said, slowly, searching for words, "he didn't look to me—he was quiet enough when I talked with him in his office down there."

"He ain't loud-mouthed, only when he's real drunk. As long as he's sober, he's fine as silk, except to anybody that tries to interfere with the Pony Express or the stage. But he ain't afraid of anything that walks. He's shot a lot of fellows, one time or another, and has just about broke up the business of rustling Express horses. But when he gets poison drunk, he's dangerous even to his best friends."

Jeff stood still, his face stern, his question more than answered. Once more a prevision of danger touched him coldly. His hair prickled under his hat.

Three figures, all unlike, yet now grouped as though brought together in an unguessed destiny, came to his mind, Chet, hurt and helpless, now on his painful eastward way; Pete Anderson, the sinister outlaw who had wounded him; Slade, relentless superintendent of the Pony Express.

He looked about him, at the barren land to which he had come. The bleak little station, the brown, sun-blasted slopes, the sharp-cut buttes, etched in sunset light, alike seemed hard and hateful. He felt, at the moment, as helpless and alone as he had felt when his father and mother died. The world once more became a dark, unfriendly place.

He looked then at his hearty, rough-and-ready partner; the moment passed. The squat log station turned home-like again; the Pony Express was Adventure and Romance. He forced a grin.

"What're you going to dish out for supper, Jack?" he demanded. "Same old stuff? Can't we have something different, for once?"

"Could if them bullwhackers would haul it out here," Lacy retorted, with a good-natured grimace. "But you ain't at the Patee House now, boy. This is the Mud Springs House! I *did* get something special today, though. Come and look."

Jeff followed him into the dusky, dirt-floored room. Lacy took a tin pail from a shelf and proudly held it out.

"Jeewhillikens! I didn't suppose plums was ripe yet! Where'd you get 'em?"

"Up yonder about a quarter of a mile, in a draw. How'll we have them?"

"Got plenty sugar?"

"I reckon there's quite a little in the sack."

"Let's stew 'em, then, with loads of sugar. I'll start the fire."

"Suits me. I'll go feed the stock."

Jeff had the stove hot and a pile of cedar wood chopped by the time Lacy came back. They cooked supper, then played checkers by lantern light a while before turning into their bunks.

As the days passed, the sunlight slanted more and more sharply through the doorway of the Mud Springs station. The buffalo grass, brown since midsummer, shrank closer to the cold dry hills. The dwarf plum trees in the coulees turned from dull green to red and brown, then all at once stood huddled, leafless. The buttes along the Platte, as Jeff passed them on his rides to and from Fort Laramie, stood outlined against a sky of softened blue. It was autumn, autumn of 1860.

Back in the States, a political campaign was closing, full of portent. North and South, uneasy, distrustful, watching each other, waited. Out on the high plains and in the sagebrush country powerful Indian tribes—the Sioux, the Arapahoes, the Cheyennes, wary, distrustful, watched the growing white invasion of their hunting lands, and waited.

The Pony Express was known now, East and West, as the surest, speediest carrier across the troubled continent. The silk-wrapped packets of tissue-paper letters and dispatches in the battered mochilas were getting thicker as the Express built up a reputation for fast, regular runs. Sun-blasted deserts, high mountain ranges, sagebrush wastes, wind-whipped short-grass plains, the menace of Indians, the jealous rivalry of the Butterfield stage line on the far southern route—the Pony Express was running despite them all.

Now, just ahead, another hazard loomed. Winter was coming—the drifting snows, the cruel storms, the bitter cold of the high plains and the intermountain country.

Jeff's shadow in the late October noonday was long on the bare, hoof-marked ground in front of the Mud Springs station. He finished reading the letter Lacy had handed him and paced a few short turns, easing his muscles after a hundred miles in the saddle. Southward, down the Julesburg trail, Bill Johnson was going out of sight, carrying the mochila Jeff had brought in from Laramie. Lacy spoke from the open doorway:

"What's the word, Jeff? How's your brother making it, that is, if that was about him. Bill thought it probably was."

Anxiety was in Jeff's voice. "He isn't getting along very well. They took that bullet out, and the place healed up, but there's still something the matter with his right side. He can't ride yet; tried it and couldn't hardly get up into the saddle. Doctor told him not to try it anymore for a while."

"That's tough, sure. He was figuring on coming back out here, wasn't he?"

"Yes. Slade told him he'd take him on again, when he got well." Jeff's face darkened as he thought of Chet, who loved to ride, unable to swing into the saddle. His hand unconsciously stole to the holster that still held the Colt he had carried on his long ride from Laramie. "Queer nobody ever sees or hears anything more about Pete Anderson. I'd like to run into him, just once," he said, meaningly.

"He may be in Texas by this time," Lacy suggested. "Nobody seems to be bothering the Express anymore; my guess is that Anderson has cleared out for good."

Jeff had no words for the instinctive dissent he felt.

"What's the news from the Fort, Jeff?" Lacy asked. There had been little chance for conversation in the scrambled moment in which Jeff had arrived and Bill departed.

"I didn't get any news. The Indians are quiet, and so is everything else. What'd Bill have to say? Julesburg's the place to get news."

"Well," Lacy began, importantly, "Bill says they're going to make a special run with the election returns."

"Clear through, you mean?"

"Yeah, from one end of the wire to the other—Fort Kearny to Fort Churchill. They're out to break the record."

Jeff by this time was standing close to his partner, he had forgotten about being tired. "When's the election?"

"First Tuesday in November, whenever that is." Lacy dived into the station and came out quickly, holding a tiny calendar. "November sixth, that's a week from tomorrow."

"Well, I'll try to do my part, if they want a fast run.

But don't skimp the ponies on feed, Jack. Give 'em a few extra dippers of oats."

"Think I don't know how to feed?" Lacy retorted, edgily. "Come out and look 'em over. See if they ain't in good shape right now."

Jeff, grinning because he had piqued Lacy so easily, followed him to the stable. There, in the squat log building, stood four Express horses. The one Jeff had ridden in from the west was stained with sweat; the sleek coats and well-carded manes and tails of the others showed that Lacy knew how to use brush and currycomb. The herby, pungent smell of prairie hay scented the stable as the horses and the seldom-used mules munched along the manger row.

"A stationman has a great life," Lacy grumbled, "with the riders hollering for him to sling in more feed and the superintendent telling him to make supplies go as far as he can." He raised the lid of a wooden bin and noted the contents. "D'you know, Jeff," he went on, "it's a fright the way this feed costs. This corn and oats was freighted all the way from St. Joe—I'll bet it cost Russell, Majors, and Waddell ten cents a pound just to haul it out here, besides whatever they had to pay for it back there. We've still got some of the wild hay that was cut down in the river bottom this summer. When that runs out, I reckon they'll have to freight in some from back East."

"Well, you don't have to pay for it," Jeff chaffed, "and I don't want you to starve these nags. Not Mack, anyway." He rubbed the rangy black's nose. "For a fast run, I reckon Mack's the one I better start with, that day. What d'you think?"

"He's about the best of the bunch. I'd take him, or Pie-face." He glanced at the sweat-marked bay Jeff had ridden in.

"Did Bill have any more news?" Jeff asked, as they went back to the cabin.

"No, nothing much. Said the rush to the Pike's Peak diggings is slowing up. Heavy travel on the stage East, he said, people getting out of the mountains before winter comes. Good deal of dust coming out by stage—ten thousand dollars worth day before yesterday."

Jeff had thought little about the election, but the order for a special run brought it sharply to his mind. "Who you reckon will be elected, Jack?" he demanded.

"How do I know? I'm buried alive here, you might say. Don't see anybody but you and Bill, and twice a month the stage driver. I haven't seen a newspaper since that one Bill fetched up from Julesburg a couple of weeks ago, and it was a month old when he got hold of it. I reckon Douglas will get it; hope so, anyhow."

"I hope Abe Lincoln gets it," Jeff returned.

"That long-legged rail splitter! He'd make a fine President, wouldn't he? Ugly as a mud fence!"

"He's not, either!" Jeff's eyes flashed. He faced Lacy with hands unconsciously clenched. "Don't talk that way about him!"

"Keep your shirt on," Lacy said, coldly. "No use for us to get worked up. It'll all be settled without any of our say-so. What makes you think so much of Lincoln?" he added, curiously.

Fragments of talk heard back in Missouri, bits of scanty

newspaper reading had formed a picture in Jeff's mind. It was real to him, but he found it hard to explain.

"Well," he began, "he was a poor boy. He lived in a log cabin, and he had to work mighty hard to get any kind of a start. He could outrassle any of his crowd. And he was so honest he walked three or four miles to give back a few cents to some woman, after he'd made a mistake in change when he was clerking in a store. I bet you he's all right!"

Lacy's lips twitched with amusement.

"What's so funny?" Jeff demanded.

Lacy's glance went round the room—the dirt floor, the rusty sheet-iron stove, the log walls hung with scanty, battered cooking utensils and ropes and saddles, the stray wisps of dry grass sticking down between the roof-poles. "I just happened to think," he drawled, "that if being poor and living in a log house helps a fellow so much, why maybe—"

"Somebody's coming yonder," Jeff interrupted.

Lacy instantly joined him in the doorway; their distance-trained eyes peered south.

The eastbound Pony Express trail ran almost due south from Mud Springs. The farthest point of the trail that could be seen from the station was a mile away. There, sharp against the skyline, an approaching horseman showed for a moment, then disappeared as the trail dipped into lower ground. The trail was little traveled. The boys stood watching. Soon, nearer, the rider showed again, coming on at a gallop.

"Looks like Slade," Jeff said.

"It *is* Slade," Lacy exclaimed.

"Don't forget to call him Captain," Jeff warned, low-voiced, as the rider neared.

"I know enough for that," his companion muttered.

"Hello, boys! How's everything?" Slade hailed.

"All right, Captain," they replied as one, their eyes on the muscular, hard-faced man who swung lightly to the ground. He tied his horse to a ring in the log wall of the station, and faced the boys.

"We're going to run a special mochila through from Fort Kearny with the election returns," he announced. He spoke almost gently. "It will probably leave on November seventh. I want you to put it through without a minute's unnecessary delay." His eyes, keen, and in that moment almost genial, flicked Jeff.

"All right, sir," Jeff replied.

"We'll be on the lookout," Lacy added, quickly.

Jeff, as he spoke, gave Slade look for look, yet not quite levelly; his unwillingly fascinated gaze sought Slade's vest, half-revealed by his unbuttoned jacket. Was that withered ear in one of those pockets?

"You boys have some pay coming," Slade continued. "Let's go inside." He led the way. Lacy slid a chair forward. Slade unbuckled his gun belt and laid it on the table. The chair he took, Jeff noted, faced the door; the guns in the holsters were never far from his hands. Next he unbuckled a money belt; it sagged in his grasp and lay heavy beside the guns.

"Here you are, Lacy," he said, as he opened the belt. He deftly stacked a little pile of coin and slid it across the rough planks. "Sign this receipt, will you?" There were seven gold eagles and a five-dollar piece in Lacy's stack.

"Next." Slade spoke briskly. His swift fingers formed another stack; he looked at Jeff. There were twelve eagles

83

and a five-dollar piece—a month's wages for a Pony Express rider—in the stack he shoved across the table.

Jeff hastily signed the receipt and took the coins. Slade replaced his money belt and put on his guns. His glance once more rested on Jeff. "Have you heard from your brother lately?" he asked.

Jeff told him about the letter that had just come.

"That may turn out all right yet," Slade said, in a tone of kindly assurance. "Gunshot wounds are uncertain, but I've seen worse-looking cases than your brother get well. We'll hope for the best."

He got up and paced about the room. "How are you getting along?" he demanded. "Anything going wrong? Anybody been bothering you?"

"No, sir," they both assured him.

"How are your supplies holding out?"

"We've got grub enough for a couple of weeks, sir," Lacy answered. "The wood is getting low, and so is the grain."

"I'll send a load of each up in a few days."

He stepped lightly to the door and outside. The boys followed him. The three stood there a moment in silence, in the afternoon's cool, hard light.

"Ever see a revolver like this?" Slade asked, drawing a small gun from one of his holsters.

Lacy, standing closer than Jeff, shook his head. "Don't think I ever did, sir. What kind is it?"

"A Smith and Wesson twenty-two. Newest thing out. Take a look at it."

He held out the gun. Lacy took it. Jeff stepped closer; he had never seen a revolver like that.

84

"Here's the way it works," Slade explained. He took the gun and broke it open. "See, the frame is hinged. The barrel tips up. You slip the cylinder off—like this—to load. Look at the cartridges."

He took a small box from his pocket and showed the boys the first metallic cartridges they had ever seen.

"Say, that's mighty neat!" Jeff exclaimed.

"Let's see you shoot it once, Captain," Lacy suggested.

Slade looked about, and picked up a small block of wood. He examined the revolver, closed it, and stuck it into his holster. Then he tossed the block into the air.

So quick was his hand that Jeff, watching, did not see him draw. Nor did Lacy. But the gun sounded; the block jumped and split in two. The gun cracked again, and the larger fragment of the block spun sharply in midair as a second bullet hit it.

"Great work!" Lacy applauded.

"That's fine shooting, sir," Jeff said. "But how in the world do you manage to draw so quick? I was watching, but all I could see was a kind of blur, then you were taking aim!"

"That takes practice," Slade explained, not displeased at Jeff's interest. "I worked a long time at that. You could learn to do it, if you tried hard enough. One part of the trick is to have your gun loose in your holster. Slip it in easily, don't jam it down. And whenever you have been carrying a gun for quite a while, especially on horseback, and think the moment is coming when you might want to use it quickly, loosen it in the holster, so you're sure it isn't sticking to the leather. That will give you a fraction of a second's advantage on the draw, which sometimes is enough

85

to make all the difference in the world. . . . This gun is too light, really, but I like the way it loads." He replaced it in his holster and untied his horse.

"Don't forget, I want good time on that special run," he added, in almost silky tones, as he swung into the saddle.

"We'll do our best, Captain."

With no other word, without a backward glance, Slade took the trail toward Fort Laramie.

Noon of November 7, 1860, at Fort Kearny. Mose Sydenham's store was full of men. This little sod house was notion store, post office, and, just lately, something more. Something new, thrilling. The soldiers and civilians wedged into the place were all watching the railed-off corner where a rough table held telegraph instruments and batteries.

A wire from Omaha, strung along the Platte bottoms on green cottonwood poles, had reached Fort Kearny less than a week before. The commandant hemmed and hawed about assigning room for a telegraph office in any of the military buildings at the fort. So Sydenham had cleared a space in one corner of his own little establishment. Here now, while the tense crowd waited, Ellsworth, the operator, sat at his key.

Those who could not wedge their way into the store stood grouped outside in front. "He'll have a good day to start," suggested one man to another beside him, sniffing the mild air. "Yes, but this is a weather-breeder," returned the other, glancing at the tall flagstaff where the United States flag hung limp, outlined against an overcast sky.

Like others of the group, they watched with friendly eyes

a youth who stood there holding a horse. Bronzed, lithe, alert the lad; slim, trim, eager the horse. The lad wore buckskin; the handle of a Colt's revolver showed in his holster, the tan mochila of the Pony Express was fitted over his horse's saddle. Narrow red and white and blue ribbons dangled from saddle and bridle; a bow of ribbons showed on the lad's arm.

Inside, the sounder on the table clicked and chattered. Ellsworth scribbled on sheets of tissue. The jammed room was hushed, no sound came but the sharp staccato of the key and the rustle of tissue paper. Suddenly Ellsworth got up. His voice trembled: "Lincoln is elected!"

A stir, a murmur, ran through the crowd. No cheers. Cool heads had advised against any demonstration, no matter what news the wire brought. Some faces darkened, some lit up with thankfulness. The air was tense.

Ellsworth pushed through the crowd to the door; the division agent of the Pony Express went with him. The agent hurried out to the waiting horse and rider. He stuffed a sheaf of tissue-paper messages into one of the mochila's compartments, locked it, and pocketed the key. "Let 'er go, Jim," he said. "Lively, now!"

The lad swung into the saddle and the horse bounded away. Now a cheer broke from the crowd. Feeling was high and divided about the election; they all admired the Pony Express.

Ellsworth went back to his key. He called Omaha, got a response, and clicked off a message for the Eastern press:

"Fort Kearny, Wed. Nov. 7
"An extra Pony Express with the election returns for California

87

left here for Fort Churchill at 1 o'clock today. It took also a considerable number of private telegrams. Both horse and rider were decorated with ribbons, etc., and they departed amid the cheers of a large gathering. This run is expected to be quicker than any ever yet made between here and the outer station of the California telegraph line. The ponies leaving St. Joseph Thursday 8th and Sunday 11th are also to make double-quick time, calling here for the latest telegraphic dates. Weather mild with tokens of rain." [5]

Jeff, pacing back and forth in front of the squat Mud Springs station late that afternoon, turned nervously to Lacy: "Jack, if they started from Kearny sometime this evening, when d'you reckon they'd get here?"

Lacy considered. "Two hundred miles to Julesburg, about sixty-five on up here. Trail ought to be in good shape now. Around noon tomorrow, or a little after, I'd say."

The lad glanced back at Fort Kearny through the dust. The crowd at Sydenham's had shrunk to a blur in the distance. He grinned as he tore off the fluttering ribbons that annoyed his horse and himself. He crouched lower over the saddle horn to lessen the air's retarding pull, and to speak: "Flint, old boy, let's go!" The rangy stride lengthened in instant response; the bursts of dust exploded faster behind the thudding hoofs.

Midforenoon of the next day, Jeff was restlessly alert. "Let's stack the grub pile for dinner pronto and get it over with," he suggested. "Bill may show up sooner than we figured."

"All right," Lacy assented. He stirred the embers in the little stove, added pine slivers and a chunk. " 'Twon't take

88

long to warm these beans. I'll fry some bacon. Want potatoes?"

"No, let 'em go this time. Make some coffee strong enough to hold up an iron wedge."

"Iron wedge? That's a new one to me, Jeff."

"That's what they say in Missouri, where I lived, when coffee is right strong—that it'll hold up an iron wedge."

"Well, I'll see what I can do."

Jeff, in the doorway, kept his eyes down the Julesburg trail. His gaze narrowed as a black dot bobbed up against the sky line on the ridge a mile away. "Somebody's coming. I bet it's Bill!" he shouted. He caught up a handful of hardtack and stuffed the pockets of his slicker. "Let that stuff go!" he exclaimed, as Lacy lingered at the stove. Together they hurried out to the stable, Jeff buckling his gun belt as he strode, Lacy carrying saddle and bridle.

"Want Mack?" Lacy asked.

"Yep."

Jeff caught up the saddle and eased it into place on the nervous black while Lacy slipped the bridle on. He drew up the latigos with quick jerks. Lacy led Mack out. Jeff followed close. A yell sounded down trail, above the quickening beat of hoofs. Another instant and Bill Johnson pulled up his panting, foam-splashed pony.

"Hi, fellows!" he greeted. "Here's your special! Lincoln's elected!"

"Good!" Jeff exclaimed. He tugged at the mochila; it stuck to Bill's saddle. Bill helped with a hard jerk; the thing came loose. They flung it over the other saddle while Lacy clung to the dancing pony's bit. Jeff strapped his

40541

RIDING WEST

slicker down behind the cantle, caught his stirrup, and swung up. Lacy let go. A clatter of hoofs on hard ground, and the election special darted out of Mud Springs.

The pair left behind waved a farewell to Jeff, then turned to the station's open door.

"Just in time for dinner, Bill," Lacy invited. "You can have the plate I put down for Jeff. He didn't have time to take a bite." He poked more wood into the stove, then straightened up with a jerk and smote his hip in vexed remembrance. "I clean forgot to put down the time," he exclaimed, pulling out his record book. " 'Twasn't much over a minute, was it, Bill?"

"Naw, hardly that much. What time is it now?" He glanced at the watch Lacy drew. "Ten eighteen? Make it in at ten fifteen and out at ten sixteen and you'll be close enough."

Jeff held the headstrong black in for a little way. Then he bent lower in the saddle and slackened the rein a trifle. "All right, Mack," he urged, "come on."

Mack shot forward in instant response. Jeff had to check him; it took more talk, a skilled hand on the rein, to settle the rangy, eager horse down into a long, ground-covering gallop that ate the trail up smoothly, swiftly.

The election was now a matter of history. North and South knew the result. Fearfully or hopefully, in winter-bound New England villages, on cotton and cane plantations swept by the soft airs of the Gulf coast, men waited to see what would come next.

A great metropolitan journal of the North looked at the matter complacently: "It is not to be supposed that the election of Abraham Lincoln as President of these United States —conspicuous and glorious triumph as it is—will at once restore the country to political harmony and quiet, though we are convinced that the agitation raised in the South will gradually and surely subside into peace." [6]

A dispatch from Washington sounded less peaceful: "A large quantity of arms was yesterday shipped from our arsenal to the South. But the place of destination remains a secret." [7]

And from Charleston, South Carolina, came this word: "There is no longer any possible doubt that the state will secede. . . . The struggle is over, and we are merely perfecting the secession arrangements." [8]

But in the far, imperial West, in new, busy ports of the Pacific littoral, in remote mining camps, in rich wide valleys beneath a genial sun, men waited yet for word of the nation's verdict. The American empire, that had grown so fast, that seemed now about to crumble into fragments, had for its best communicating tie between East and West a scanty line of bronzed young horsemen, coursing from station to lonely station through the land of sagebrush and desert, stopping not for night or day or storm or fair. Couriers of empire, these boys of the Pony Express!

Gallant the riders; the ponies fleet of foot. Yet, so vast the land to be crossed, ten days went by while a mochila was being carried on regular schedule from the Missouri River to Sacramento. This election ride was special.

For all the rangy black's toughness and bottom he was

panting and faltering when Jeff swung down at the relay station.

"Put him right through, didn't yuh?" remarked the stationman.

"Well, you know the orders."

"Sure. I got the one yuh like for yuh, Jeff."

"I see."

He was changing over mochila and slicker with quick jerks as he spoke. He caught his stirrup. The man held the raw-boned dun horse, letting go as Jeff's weight settled into the saddle. The horse snorted, bucked, then straightened out in a reaching gallop that speedily left the squat, cedar-pole station far behind. The November sun was low in the overcast sky. The ice-fringed Platte ran cold and swift between its endless sandbars on Jeff's right; the lonely trail slipped past.

He brought the "ornery" dun into the next station subdued, foam-wet, quivering. Another change, to a speedy, nervy bay. Then on, without a moment's rest.

The smell of coming storm, damp yet crisp, was borne on the night air. A chilling wind from mountain ranges pressed against horse and rider. Jeff slowly lost the high-keyed feeling that had held him up. He was cold, dizzy, dead-tired, when he slid off his gasping, faltering horse in the yellow circle of lantern light at Laramie station.

"Boy, you've been traveling!" called the stationman. "What's the news?"

Jeff tugged at the mochila. "Lincoln's elected!" he gasped.

The waiting rider, brown, slim, hard, smiled as he caught

92

the stiff square of leather and clapped it down over the fresh and fretting pony's saddle. "Here goes!" he cried, above the wind and the quick clatter of his pony's feet. Then he was gone into the black and threatening night.

Ahead in bleak darkness lay lonely stations, tiny outposts in an empty land—Horseshoe, Labonte Creek, Platte Bridge, Willow Springs, Independence Rock, Devil's Gate, and the three treacherous crossings of the icy Sweetwater in its rocky canyon. Beyond that was Ice Slough, Burnt Ranch, wind-swept South Pass, and the desolate stretch to Fort Bridger.

The West Coast was far, very far, from the rest of the nation. Word of the special mochila's progress got back to the Pony Express stations only gradually. It was night of Thursday, November 8, that Jeff brought the special into Laramie. It was the forenoon of Thursday, November 22, that he pulled into Mud Springs on one of his regular east-bound runs. Gaunt and hollow-eyed from the unending saddle grind, he slid stiffly to the ground and announced to Lacy and the waiting Bill Johnson:

"That extra got to Salt Lake in good time, anyhow!"

"Did? What was the time? Who told you?"

"Joe Jackson brung the word to Laramie. They set her down in Salt Lake City in three days and four hours from Fort Kearny."

"Going some, I'll say!"

"Good thing they had their election when they did, I reckon, if they wanted the news to get through quick," Jeff went on, wearily. "Been snowing for two days and a night when this left Salt Lake."

This was the brown, battered mochila. Bill Johnson caught it from Jeff, eased it expertly over his saddle, stepped into the leather.

"So long, fellers."

The eastbound mail, once more, was out of Mud Springs.

VIII   AN EXPRESS CHRISTMAS

"I've got enough of this!"

Jeff did not look up from the month-old newspapers he was reading. The yellow light of the lantern lit the pages outspread on the plank table.

Lacy, beside the stove, shifted his feet impatiently on the dirt floor. Jeff spoke absently. "What'd you say, Jack?"

"I say I'm fed up on this whole business!"

"What're you talking about, anyhow?"

"The blasted Pony Express. I'm sick and tired of it."

Jeff let go his paper. "What's the matter now?"

"You heard me."

Jeff waited, not knowing what to say, and Lacy went on unburdening himself.

"What's the use of staying out here in this God-forsaken hole all winter? Live on hardtack and beans—I never want to see another dish of beans!"

"Jed said he'd see if he couldn't rustle a can or two of fruit for us, next trip."

"Bah! I don't see why you're so stuck on this layout, Jeff. Ride your head off—help 'em hang up a record with the blasted election returns—what does it get you?"

"They've given us an easier schedule for the winter."

"Yeah, fifteen days from St. Joe to Sacramento, eleven days Fort Kearny to Churchill. But I'm telling you *any* schedule through here in winter will be devilish tough business. I don't believe the boys can make it."

"Jed give you a big song and dance yesterday, did he?"

Lacy reddened in the uncertain light. "I can figure out some things for myself, without any long-haired bullwhacker to help me."

"All right, then, you don't like it. What're you going to do about it?"

Lacy hesitated, then spoke fast. "Let's both quit. We've been out here long enough to get a fair stake, both of us. We can go down to Julesburg, draw what's coming to us, and maybe get a half-decent meal or two. Then we could take the stage back to God's country. Wouldn't you like to put up at the Patee House for two or three days, sleep between real sheets, and have those darky waiters bring you a six-course meal when you go into that big dining room? And you could be with your brother this winter. You and he could get something to do where you'd be together, whenever he is able to work; there's plenty of jobs back East. A lot of the Pony Express fellows are dropping out, for the winter, anyhow. What do you say?"

Silence in the small, half-lighted room. Dead silence, for a moment. Then the November wind, rising fitfully, rattled the rusty stovepipe above the sod roof. As that noise died,

96

came a sound sinister, flesh-creeping. It rang across the wind-swept hills and snow-filled coulees, the howl of a gray wolf, the savage killer that could hamstring a horse or a buffalo with one slash of its fangs.

Jeff moved uneasily in his seat; his lips tightened. He shook himself as though to throw off a weight that pressed him. His face hardened finely.

He had not heard from Chet for a month; in all that time there had not been a day when he had not thought of him, longed to be with him, to help him in some way. . . .

The door of the little stove was ajar, the blazing cedar chunks threw a wedge of light across the floor. Jeff, seeing it, thought of the slanting sunlight, like a strong hand pointing, that shone across the boards in Alexander Majors' office the day his brother signed up as Pony Express rider, and he himself had vowed that he would not rest till he, too, got on.

Phrases from that day ran through his mind. "It isn't a matter of trying to make money—we are more likely to lose. . . . If you ride the Pony Express you will have a hard part. You will be a courier of empire."

And Chet had not quit! A thrill ran through Jeff. He got up. A weight seemed to slip from him.

Again, as on that day, he stood for an instant outside himself. He heard himself say: "I'm going to stay with it."

Lacy shrugged. He leaned over and poked the fire, and threw in more wood. The stove began to hum and glow. The wind, now risen, drove sand and snow against the cabin window; it strummed and moaned across the stovepipe in the roof. Again, above the strumming wind, came the howl of a great wolf, a flesh-prickling sound in the black night.

97

Yet the tension in the room lessened. Courage, warm and vibrant, rose stronger than doubt or fear. Lacy and Jeff moved a half-step closer to each other. They felt an unspoken intimacy they had not known for days.

"Anything special in the paper?" Lacy asked, casually.

"There was a funny sort of item about a new flag down in South Carolina. Did you see it?"

"No. Read it out loud."

Jeff turned the tattered sheets under the lantern light. "From Charleston, South Carolina, news:

"THE SOUTH CAROLINA FLAG

"This glorious Flag now flies from many windows of buildings in our city, and we hope in a few days to see hundreds of them unfolding over our heads. No one at the present time can gaze on this standard of our State without feeling his heart swell with emotion, and his arm nerved and strengthened with a determination to stand by it to the last."

"What do they want a State flag for?" Jeff commented. "Ain't the Stars and Stripes good enough for them?"

"It isn't just that," Lacy said, defensively. "In the South, people stand by their home states. Why, in Virginia, where my folks live, they'd fight for the State at the drop of a hat. I don't know, now that Lincoln's elected, just what may happen. . . . What say we have a game or two before we turn in?"

"Suits me," Jeff responded. He tossed the paper aside and reached in the table for the well-thumbed checkerboard and men. The wind roared over the cabin and sand whipped against the window as they played contentedly on, late into

98

the night, looking up from the board only to replenish the hungry little stove with cedar chunks.

Bill Johnson's face was grim as he clattered in with the westbound mail next day. "Looks like the devil to pay up the line," he greeted.

"What's up?"

"Where?"

Jeff paused in the act of reaching for the mochila Bill dangled on his arm.

"Indians. A big bunch of 'em down around Cottonwood Springs. They're running the ponies off from the stations down there."

"Are they actually on the war path?" Lacy asked.

"May be by this time. I don't know. There hadn't been any real fighting when Little Yank got through with this mail. He—"

"Well," Jeff broke in, "I got to go." He jammed his old beaked cloth cap lower, and mounted. "So long, fellows."

They waved a farewell. Lacy noted the time. Two minutes had elapsed from the arrival of the mail till its departure. Anything more than that would have called for a written explanation in the station record book.

About the middle of the afternoon next day, Jeff got back to Mud Springs with the eastbound mail. He had had only a couple of hours' layover at Fort Laramie. Lacy and Bill stood outside the station; they had seen him coming.

"See any Indians?" Jeff called, as he got close.

"Not a thing. We've been on the lookout; haven't seen anything or anybody since you pulled out yesterday."

"Everything's quiet between here and Laramie," Jeff reported.

As Bill rode off down the trail, Lacy turned to Jeff: "I've changed my mind, Jeff. I'm going to stick, for a while, anyhow. I won't run away when it looks as though we might have Indian trouble."

"Good! I didn't want you to go, Jack. They'd send somebody else in here, of course, but I'd rather have a fellow I know."

A little later, as Jeff was chopping firewood beside the cabin, he sighted a horseman coming in over the Julesburg trail. He called Lacy, who was doing chores at the stable. Together they watched the approaching rider.

"It's Slade!" Lacy muttered, as the horseman neared. They stood waiting, watching.

"Hello, boys, how's everything?" the superintendent greeted.

"All right here, Captain," they both answered.

"How about the Indians down the line?" Lacy ventured. Jeff silently watched the muscular, martial figure that swung lightly to the ground.

"There won't be any trouble," Slade said. "Captain Steele and his company from the Second Infantry came out to Cottonwood from Kearny. The Indians quieted down as soon as the troops showed up."

Slade's blue-gray eyes turned on Jeff. Fun danced in them in that instant, Jeff fancied. "Been practicing the draw any lately?" the superintendent demanded, banteringly.

Jeff reddened. "Yes, sir, I have, some."

"Some!" Lacy exclaimed. "He's at it about half the time that he's here at the station, I'd say."

"He might be doing worse things than that," Slade said, looking at Jeff approvingly. "Let me see you try it."

Jeff, embarrassed, went in and buckled on his gun belt. He came back out, having first carefully loosened the heavy Colt in its holster. Then, acutely aware of the keen eyes watching him, he whipped the weapon out and brought it down on an imaginary target.

"Not bad," Slade said. "I'd keep on practicing if I were you." He stepped close to Jeff. "You'll find you can do better by having the holster a trifle further to the front," he suggested, twisting Jeff's gun belt slightly around as he spoke.

"Much obliged, sir," Jeff said, carefully noting the adjustment. "I'll remember that."

The superintendent deftly drew Jeff's weapon from its holster and balanced it expertly in his muscular, well-shaped hands. "If you're really interested in learning to be quick on the draw, you ought to have a Smith and Wesson twenty-two," he said. "It is a much lighter gun; you could handle it a great deal faster. I can get you one at the wholesale price, if you think you'd care to have it."

"How much would it cost, sir?"

"About twenty dollars. Understand, I'm not telling you to do this; it's entirely up to you. But I know you'd find it a nice gun for this kind of practice."

"I wish you'd get one for me, Captain," Jeff decided, promptly.

"All right. I'll bring you one, and a supply of cartridges the next time I go through, or if I'm not up this way soon I'll send it up by Johnson. When you get it you might practice drawing and firing at a moving target. Toss up a piece of wood—start with a good-sized chunk, and when you get so you can hit that gradually work down to smaller blocks."

With that, abruptly, Slade turned and strode out to the stable, without asking anyone to follow. The boys stayed where they were. He returned presently and addressed Lacy: "Have you looked at that black's feet lately?"

"Well—no, sir, I don't know as I have, especially."

"Keep your eyes open. He's showing quarter cracks—not bad, yet. Take him and that bay down to Julesburg tomorrow. Have them both reshod, sharp calks all around. Have the smith soak the black's feet in oil, and bring a bottle of oil back with you and rub some on his hoofs every day for a while."

"All right, Captain."

Slade untied his horse; he reached for his saddle horn, then paused in the act of mounting and again faced Jeff and Lacy.

"Don't take any strangers in for food or lodging, no matter what kind of story they put up," he admonished. His voice had now an undertone of menace; his eyes, to Jeff's startled gaze, showed darker. "Tell them to keep going, unless it's somebody you actually know. I've cleaned out most of the tough hombres between Julesburg and Rocky Ridge, but there's a few left yet—and I don't propose to have them using Express stations for hangouts. Understand?"

"Yes, sir!"

"Good day, boys."

"Good day, Captain."

"D'you reckon he notches his guns?" Jeff queried, when the superintendent was out of earshot. "I couldn't see any marks on them."

"Naw, he wouldn't bother about *that*. Why, there wouldn't hardly be room enough on his guns, unless he notched mighty fine. He's rubbed out more than twenty hombres, they say. One time he went out single-handed after four fellows that'd held up a stage. They was in a ranch house—he walked right up, kicked the door open, and cut loose. Got three of 'em right there—the last man jumped through a window and the Captain picked him off on the run."

"I reckon," Jeff said, thoughtfully, "it takes somebody about like that to keep things straight out here."

"Sure it does."

"And I reckon when he tells a fellow to do something, he'd better do it."

"You said it! Watch me hit the trail for Julesburg in the morning. I never noticed Mack's feet were starting to crack."

Short the days now, low the sun in its southern zone, crisp the short grass that clung to the frozen hills. In the mochila Bill Johnson tossed over to Jeff one December morning, as a slow dawn was creeping up, was a sheaf of tissue sheets bearing President Buchanan's last regular message to Congress. The wire had brought it to Fort Kearny, ticked it out in Sydenham's sod store; the Pony Express picked it up there. It was long, scholarly, able, a plea to the South to do nothing rash: "But may I be permitted solemnly to invoke my countrymen to pause and deliberate before they determine to destroy this, the grandest temple which has ever been dedicated to human freedom since the world began."

The Pony Express took this west on its ordinary schedule. Snow was closing down over the mountain trails. The mochila with Buchanan's message was twelve days going from Kearny to Fort Churchill.

"D'you know what a week from today is?" Lacy demanded, one gray morning, as he came in from the stable. A puff of dry, icy wind swept in with him. He kicked the door shut and knocked the snow from his boots.

"Sure, I know," Jeff replied, with a grin. "The twenty-fifth of December.. What they call Christmas, most places."

His grin was mostly on the outside; the memory of Christmastides at home, in sheltered days, came to him sharply.

But he had something. He felt in an inner pocket to be sure the letter was there. Chet had written that he was at last on the mend. By spring, early spring, he was going to come West again and get back on the Pony Express. The thought brought warmth to Jeff's heart; it was like far strains of marching music.

"We ought to do something a little special, hadn't we?" Lacy persisted.

"I'll see if I can pick up anything different in the way of grub at Laramie, next trip. . . . What'd the blacksmith say about Mack's feet? They don't look bad to me."

"He said they'd be all right, want to watch 'em a little, though."

Lacy stuffed more wood into the little stove, and spread his hands close to its sheet-iron top. "That cold goes right through me this morning, somehow. What was you saying about snow out West, Jeff?"

"Jackson said it was three feet deep through South Pass and along Rocky Ridge."

"I reckon that time with the election special will hold 'em for a while, Jeff. Six days and twenty-one hours from Kearny to Churchill!" [10]

"I reckon it will. And if we get a stemwinder of a storm through here, we'll be lucky to keep the mail moving at all."

Christmas morning at Mud Springs. The searing cold, stealing into the log station as the banked fire burned faint and fainter in the little stove, drove Jeff out of his bunk while the single frosted windowpane was no more than gray with coming dawn. He pulled on his boots, his sheep-lined coat, rekindled the fire with cedar slivers, shook Lacy.

"Pile out of there, slow poke. See what Santa Claus brought you."

"G'wan. The old boy wouldn't hit the trail out this far. Got too much sense, I'll bet."

But Lacy crawled out. He tried to pull his boots on. Something hard was in one toe. A small, brown-paper package. He tore it open, glancing queerly at Jeff, who stood watching.

"Well, I'll be—where'd you get that?" He held up a pocketknife, turning it in his palm, a shiny, keen-looking knife, three-bladed.

"Sutler's store, Laramie."

"You couldn't have hit me better. . . . Well, I got a little something for you."

From behind a seldom-used saddle on the wall, Lacy brought out a larger, shapeless package, handed it to Jeff, and stood by while he unwrapped it. A cap of beaver fur, brown, glossy.

Jeff held it, stroked the fur, tried it on, pulling it down far over his ears. "That—that feels great," he said, in a voice suddenly husky. "Where'd you get it?"

"Bill got it from an Indian down at Julesburg; I told him to be on the lookout."

The winter wind, never long still on the high plains, was rising. It whined across the stovepipe in the roof, it tore through the doorway as Lacy went out to do the chores—a bleak wind, whipping up the powdery snow. Snow and sand whirled the day long around the log station. But inside it was Christmas—Christmas of 1860, the one Christmas the Pony Express was to know.

IX AN OVERNIGHT GUEST

BILL JOHNSON might have been a wraith, so silently he rode up through the powdery, hoof-muffling snow. His warning whoop, from down trail, had brought Jeff and Lacy out; they stood in front of the station with saddled pony and lantern.

"You have any Christmas?" Bill greeted, as he pulled up, ignoring their pointed, jabbing inquiry into his reason for being more than a day late.

"Sure did," Jeff replied. "Buffalo ribs and gravy, and real bread!"

"G'wan! Where'd you get any bread?"

"Stationman at Laramie sent us a loaf," Lacy explained, "along with a chunk of buffalo. And we had a glass of jelly. Boy, I'm telling you that bread and jelly hit the spot!"

They slipped the mochila on the other saddle automatically as they talked. Jeff tied his muffler, pulled his new fur cap lower. He was reaching for his stirrup when the change in Bill's voice made him turn.

"They was one rider didn't have no Christmas."

"How you mean?"

"That's why the mail's late, fellers. A rider got off the trail in a storm east o' Kearny. Day before Christmas. He was just a new man, a German. He was froze when they found him." [11]

"Dead?"

"Dead as a doornail. You know, it was cold as blazes out here, too, time that storm went through. I like to froze, myself."

"This the mochiler he had?"

"Yeah, same one, they said. . . . Watch yourself, old man."

Jeff stepped into the leather. The mochila was still a little warm from Bill's body; faint warmth from the pony came up under his wolfskin chaps. The pony's breath and his own were white in the dim moonlight.

When he had ridden a little way he glanced back. The station was a vague blot in the whiteness, a moon-haloed wisp of smoke hovering over it. He could guess what was going on inside. Lacy poking up the fire, Bill stretching his hands out to the stove from the ease of the best chair, the one with the cowhide seat, hair side up. The battered lantern's yellow light on the table. Bill would be telling Lacy some more about the rider who froze to death. A new man, Jeff reflected.

108

Well, with a lot of the old riders dropping out, of course there'd be green ones coming in. But it looked like the pony would have known the trail. Still—sometimes a storm hit hard and sudden-like, and if a man didn't watch himself—

Jeff drew himself closer inside his coat. He raised and dropped himself in the stirrups. He threshed his arms about; he talked to Pieface, and pushed him to a gallop for short stretches where some of the snow was blown off the trail. In deeper snow the best he could get out of his pony was a slow trot or a plunging walk. Jeff knew, from bitter experience, how far it was from Mud Springs to Laramie on a midwinter night.

He yelled when the first relay station showed ahead, a dim, snow-banked shanty in the Platte bottoms, the sandbars of the wide river bed lying dark to north of it. Nobody came out; no light showed as he rode up. He kicked and pounded the door; a voice answered, and the stationman struggled into his boots and coat. Jeff waited inside, in the grateful stuffy warmth, in the familiar smell of leather and horse blankets, while a fresh pony was saddled. There was a brief word about the rider who froze to death. Then Jeff went on. It was, the man said, four o'clock in the morning.

The slow winter dawn came, hours later. The buttes, looking lower because snow was drifted deep along their eastern sides, stood out hard and clear. The sun came up unwarmingly. The wind, piercing cold, began to blow.

Another relay station, another change, another long grind in the saddle, over a wind-drifted trail that climbed higher and higher into the foothills. The pony was white with frost, Jeff was numb with cold, his muffler a mat of ice across his nostrils, when he slid stiffly out of the saddle late that afternoon at Fort Laramie.

"White spot on your face, there, old man," warned Jackson, the waiting rider. He caught up a handful of snow, held it against Jeff's cheek.

"That'll be all right. I'll fix it," Jeff mumbled. "Been kind of a cold trip. Watch yourself, Joe—one rider froze to death this trip, east o' Kearny."

"Did? Huh! Well, I'll try to keep awake. This ain't the time o' year to take a nap in the saddle. 'Tain't healthy. So long."

And he was off, his pony's feet sending up a skurry of dry snow along the drifted trail, over which a storm-set evening was darkening.

A Postmaster General of the United States had declared, three years before, that regular mail service could never be established over the central route. The winters were too cold; the snows too deep. Now, because of the nerve of wire-tough Pony Express riders, San Francisco was able to send this complacent message east:

"San Francisco, Dec. 15.
"Via Pony Express and Ft. Kearny:
"The patronage of the Express is increasing under the influence of regular trips. The last outgoing Express took 175 letters from San Francisco and 34 from Sacramento, many of them double letters paying five dollars each. Today the Express will take about 85 letters from San Francisco."

Jeff drank hot coffee, pulled off his outer clothing, crawled into a bunk, and slept till midforenoon of the next day. Then, after a hearty meal, he felt ready for anything.

"Weather turned off fine," the stationman announced. "You'll have it easy, going back."

The wind had gone down. The air was milder. Laramie Peak loomed with softened outlines.

The mail from the West got in a little after noon. Jeff took it eastward. The pony galloped over wind-swept stretches where the dry snow was no more than fetlock-deep, then plodded and lunged through dreary wastes where crusted drifts came up to the stirrups.

Looking back, Jeff saw a gray veil hiding the crest of Laramie Peak, a veil that slipped lower and lower over the mountain's stony shoulders. A haze was shortening his view in all directions. The air was soft and still. The haze thickened into early night. He pushed on, hour after hour, down the desolate trail.

He was a little way out of the last relay station, on the final stretch to Mud Springs, when an eerie sound, like a giant's sigh, breathed through the silence. The air about him lifted strangely. Then, from behind, he heard a murmur, a rustle, quickening to a roar. Then the blizzard struck. Its blast was like an avalanche. Snow of incredible fineness instantly swirled in blinding clouds.

Jeff drew his cap lower, pulled his heavy muffler tight around his neck and across his face. The snow powder sifted through the folds; he felt its icy touch on mouth and nose.

He let the reins hang on the saddle horn; no guidance of his could keep the trail. The pony lowered its head and trotted doggedly through the muffling swirl. The roaring storm deafened them.

Jeff beat himself with his arms, he rose in the stirrups

and settled back hard, but his blood flowed slower and slower. Snow, wind, cold—he had met them, defied them on many a long ride. Never such a savage, stinging blast. The wind shrieked like a giant in pain. The choking fineness of the snow, the piercing cold benumbed him.

He lost his sense of place and distance. Time stood still; he had no notion how long the storm had been roaring. He thought dully of the new rider who had lost his way east of Fort Kearny. Again he swung his arms, again he rose in the stirrups and settled back, but his motions had no force. As he rode on, he was less and less aware of the cold. He told himself that a little nap in the saddle, after his long ride, was what he needed. The pony, drifting before the blast, its head down, its ears caked, its hair matted with powdery snow, would keep the trail. He drooped in the saddle. . . .

The wind slackened for a moment. The pony lifted its head and whinnied. Jeff's heart bounded; his blood ran faster. He saw, just ahead, the snow-shrouded figure of a horse and rider, moving slowly down the wind. He forced his pony alongside the other.

"Where you bound for?" he called, through the quickening roar of the storm.

The shrouded rider started in his seat; it seemed to Jeff that he fumbled at his belt.

"Who in blazes are you?" he demanded.

"Pony Express rider, heading for Mud Springs."

"This the trail?"

"Don't know. Letting my horse go. Reckon he'll make it," Jeff shouted.

The other made no reply. The snow-blown ponies plodded on down-wind.

Jeff felt fresh strength. New life tingled painfully in his fingers and toes. Soon, too, in another lull of the wind, he glimpsed a stunted pine tree.

"I know where we are now," he called to his companion. " 'Bout a mile more to the station."

The other, humped over in his saddle, said not a word. With stirrups almost touching they rode up to the snow-whipped little cabin. Jeff whooped as loud as he could. He slid out of the saddle then, tottered over to the door, kicked it with numbed feet. "Lacy!" he shouted. "It's me! Jeff! Open up!"

"All right!" a voice answered.

A moment or two and the bar was drawn; the door swung back. Lacy, with tousled head and blinking eyes stood there holding a lantern.

"Whew!" he ejaculated, "I never looked for you tonight. Get in here, quick. I'll get some more clothes on in a minute and put the pony up."

"There's a fellow out there," Jeff said, guardedly, as he clumped through the doorway. "We'd better take him in, hadn't we? It's bad, out. I thought a time or two I wouldn't make it. Bill don't want to start on tonight."

Lacy, peering out, saw the mounted man.

"Who is it?" he muttered, turning back, and pushing the door shut. "Where'd he come from?"

"I don't know—overtook him on the trail. Whoever he is, he's a goner if he stays out much longer. It's getting worse right along."

"Well—if you want to—"

Jeff clumped out into the white maelstrom. "Come on in!" he shouted.

"Guess I will." The man slid down stiffly. "What about my horse?"

"We'll put it in the stable. Come on in."

Jeff stripped the icy mochila from his saddle and led the way into the station. The lantern's light now showed Bill Johnson sitting on the edge of his bunk, struggling with his boots.

"How is she, Jeff?" he called.

"Worse I ever saw. Don't try it tonight. The mail's ahead of schedule, anyhow. I was out when she hit, and had to keep coming, but I wouldn't start out in it."

Bill pondered, holding his second boot in his hands. "Guess I'll let 'er go till daylight," he decided.

Lacy turned up his coat collar, pulled his cap down, picked up the lantern, and started out. The stranger, his hawklike face glistening with melting snow, stepped after him. "I'll help you," he muttered.

Bill put on his other boot. He stirred the fire and threw in more wood. "Who is that hombre, Jeff?" he asked.

"Don't know him from Adam. Overtook him on the trail somewhere this side of Chimney Rock. I wouldn't turn an Indian away, even, a night like this."

Lacy and the stranger presently came back from the stable. The lantern light showed the unknown guest as young, lean, dark, hard-favored. He shook the snow from his shoulders and stood by the glowing stove. He did not at once unbutton his coat. Jeff, close to the opposite side of the stove, noted the bulge of a gun belt under the coat as the two stood there, warming. Save for the strumming wind and crackling fire, there was a little space of uneasy silence in the small, half-lighted room.

"What time is it, Jack?" Jeff asked.

Lacy, on the edge of his bunk, pulled his watch. "Five minutes till twelve. Might as well turn in, whenever you fellows get thawed out. We'll have to double up—I'll crawl in with Bill." He did.

The glowing stove was luxury supreme to Jeff. The guest, too, drew an appreciative sigh as he hovered wordless beside it. At last he spoke: "Any time you say, pard."

"All right, let's go." Jeff replied.

They pulled off their boots, their coats and vests. Jeff got in first, at the other's suggestion. The lantern had been blown out; only a faint light came from the closed stove. He heard the stranger lay his gun belt gently on the floor within reach, before easing himself under the blanket.

Jeff, though tired, felt strangely alert. He lay awake for a time, while the storm whipped the stanch little cabin till it shook and shivered, and cold crept into the room as the fire burned lower. Some sixth sense told him that his unstirring bunk mate was not asleep. But at last Jeff slept soundly.

He roused at a thumping noise. Lacy was stamping into his boots. Daylight showed in the frosted window. The stranger was up, he had made his morning toilet by donning boots, gun belt, and fur-lined coat; he was coaxing a blaze in the little stove.

"Colder than blue blazes," Lacy announced, his breath showing white. "And still blowing," he added, needlessly, as the high, icy note of the strumming wind rose to a shriek above the snow-whipped cabin.

Jeff got up, and shook Bill out. All four stood close to the stove till the fire got going strong. Then Lacy rigged himself for outdoors. "I'll tend to the chores first thing," he said. "Some of you fellows can start getting breakfast if you want to."

"I'll go out with you, Jack," Bill Johnson decided. "We'll see what you fellows can cook up." He grinned impartially at Jeff and the stranger; then the plank door slammed behind him as he followed Lacy out into the whirling snow.

"Looks like they're putting it up to you and me," Jeff remarked, cheerfully. "Breakfasts at Mud Springs are all about alike, and nothing to brag on."

The tall stranger's hard face remained impassive. "Anything will do me," he said charily, as he saw Jeff waiting for some reply.

"Well, I'll put the coffee on, and fix some potatoes," Jeff said. He broke thick ice in the water pail, filled the coffee pot, and got some potatoes from a small, blanket-covered pit in a corner of the cabin. "You might slice off some bacon, if you will."

"Sure."

Jeff was peeling potatoes when the stranger held out the frying pan for his inspection. "Enough?"

"Yeah, I reckon that'll do." The feel of something wrong ran along Jeff's nerves as his quick glance caught the taut

116

bitterness of the weather-beaten face, the shifty look in the powder-gray eyes.

The man set the frying pan on the glowing stove, and tossed his tousled hair back from his eyes with a jerk of his head. Jeff had a glimpse of a white scar that lay across his temple. Then he knew!

"You're Pete Anderson!" he cried. "You shot my brother!" His muscles tightened; he drew himself together. "I'll settle with you!" He sprang at the man.

Anderson drew back lithely. His flinty face did not change; his beady eyes flickered wickedly. He did not reach for the guns in his belt. He lashed a savage jab of his hard fist as Jeff rushed in. It caught Jeff on the point of the chin, checking his rush, so that he poised an instant without motion. Then his arms sagged, his knees bent; he fell face forward to the floor. . . .

He was struggling to his feet when the door opened a couple of minutes later and Lacy and Bill came in. This second whiff of bitter-cold air cleared his brain. "Where'd he go?" he demanded. "Get after him, quick!"

"What's the matter, Jeff?"

"That fellow! It's Pete Anderson! Where'd he go?"

Bill Johnson put out a steadying hand. "Easy, Jeff. We didn't see him. Did he slug you?"

"What makes you think it's Anderson?" Lacy asked.

Jeff sat down, his knees shaky. He spoke impetuously. "He'll get clear away if we don't get a move on! I tell you, it's Anderson, the fellow that shot Chet! I saw the scar on his forehead. Come on!" He got up, found his gun belt, buckled it on, pulled on coat and cap.

117

A trifle slowly, Lacy and Bill put on their guns. Jeff led the way to the stable, through the blasting snow. The stable door was banging in the wind. They stepped gingerly through the doorway.

"His horse is gone!" Lacy exclaimed.

"Sure," Bill agreed, sarcastically. "You don't reckon he'd go off afoot, do you?"

"Let's saddle up and get after him!" Jeff urged.

Bill stepped to the doorway. He drew Jeff to his side. "Look out there," he directed.

A blast of powdery snow shot up to hide the cabin from their sight. The wind's roar rose to a shriek.

"You couldn't trail an elephant in that," Bill said, reasonably. "Tracks 'ud fill faster 'n a fellow made 'em. No chance. He's gone. Let him go. I don't know as I hanker to get very close to that hombre, again, anyhow. And he'll be lucky if he don't freeze to death."

"You're dead right, Bill," said Lacy.

Jeff felt his aching jaw. "I reckon that's so," he agreed, reluctantly. "We couldn't trail him in this. But I—" He left it unfinished.

They battled back to the cabin and had breakfast. Jeff, somewhat against his will, had to recount every detail of his overtaking the outlaw on the trail the night before, and of their encounter of the morning.

"He'll come back some night and clean out the stable," Lacy predicted, gloomily.

"Don't think he'll bother you. That hombre goes after bigger game than horses," Bill Johnson said. "He sure looked like a tough bird."

118

Jeff ran his fingers over his jaw and made no comment.

By midafternoon the wind's note sounded less loudly across the stovepipe in the roof. "She's going down," Lacy confirmed, coming in with a double armful of wood from the stack in the lee of the cabin. "But the snow's still sifting along right lively."

"Well, I'm a-going to sift out for Julesburg with that mail," Bill declared. "What's a little snow, more or less?"

Jeff stepped out to look around. The wind was an icy knife; snow was crawling along over the crusts in strands like woolly ropes.

"You're crazy, Bill," he said, as he went back inside and hastily slammed the door.

"Sure, I know it. Wouldn't be on the Express in wintertime if I wasn't. But I'm going, allee samee."

Lacy brought a pony around. The mochila was taken down from a peg on the cabin wall and slapped onto the saddle. Lacy and Jeff gave Bill a few chaffing words of advice, waved him farewell as he plunged away, then ducked back into the station.

Jeff, cramming the stove with wood, caught Lacy looking at him quizzically. "I haven't got thawed out yet from that ride last night, Jack," he grinned, "and I'm going to get good and warm, no matter if wood costs a hundred dollars a cord!"

"Hop to it," Lacy acquiesced. "I didn't say a word."

Toward sunset the wind went down. The cold became intense. The humped-up ponies and mules would not drink when Lacy led them over crusted snow down to the hole he had chopped through the ice at the spring. The bucket of water Jeff brought from the spring to the cabin steamed like hot water. The air seemed to sear his face and eyeballs as he hurried along.

"Wish we had a thermometer," he remarked, as Lacy came stamping in from the stable, his muffler white around his mouth. "How cold you reckon it is?"

"Forty below, I bet. Let me show you something."

He took a dipperful of water, stepped out, and threw it high in air with a sweeping motion. The spray froze in mid-air and rattled down like hail on the snow crust.

"Well, that beats my time!" Jeff exclaimed. He had known hard winter before, but this was the cold of the high plains. "Bill will have a cold old trip," he added, thoughtfully.

"It won't be a warm one."

But they slept warm that night, getting up a few times to cram the little stove. Next morning the easier feeling in the air told them that the crest of the cold had passed.

There was little to do; no place to go. The stable chores were light, the monotonous job of cooking was simple. They had nothing fresh to read and were tired of checkers. Jeff was keyed to restlessness, he longed to see Chet, he was still wrought up over his encounter with Pete Anderson. When he jested with Lacy his merriment was only on the surface. Lacy, too, was out of sorts. The slow round of a station keeper's job was becoming too much for his patience.

The only piece of reading matter in the cabin was a tattered copy of the *Chicago Tribune,* weeks out of date. Jeff had read it all, even the fine-type advertisements. Now in boredom he scanned the paper again while Lacy was getting supper.

"Here, Jack," he called, "this might be a chance for you, if you want another job."

"What is it?"

Jeff read the advertisement aloud: "A good cook wanted, one who understands making bread and pastry, and is well recommended, by a family of the highest responsibility. Wages ten dollars a month. Apply after five in the afternoon, at number nine West Twelfth Street."

"Huh!"

"I don't know, though," Jeff chaffed, "maybe you'd better not try for it, after all. This says a *good* cook, well recommended—"

Lacy, stirring potatoes in the frying pan, straightened up with a jerk. His face reddened with a heat not from the glowing stove. He kicked the stove door open and dumped the contents of the pan into the fire. "If you don't like the way I cook," he snapped, "try it yourself for a change. I'm through!"

"Oh, here, now, you needn't get sore," Jeff protested. "I was just joking."

Lacy stalked over to his bunk and sat down without so much as glancing at his cabin mate.

Jeff waited a few minutes, holding the paper under the lantern light, pretending to read. Then he tossed it aside and looked over the prospect for supper. There was hardtack, stacked on a plate, a platter of fried bacon, the warmed-over beans left from dinner, coffee, simmering and losing its best flavor by being too long in the making.

"Come on, Jack," he called, "let's eat what's here."

"Eat, if you feel like it. I don't want any supper."

Jeff ate some of the tiresome food, but there was little good in it for him. The air of the room vibrated with ill-feeling.

When he was through, Jeff put the things away, washed his dish or two, and tried to read some more. He could not get his mind on the paper. A while he sat firmly, doing nothing. Then he banked the fire, undressed, blew out the lantern, and crawled into his bunk. Lacy was already under the blankets in his own sleeping place.

Almost at once Jeff went to sleep, but in the middle of the night he woke, not knowing at first what was heavy on his mind. Then the recollection of his partner's dourness came back to him.

He tried to go back to sleep, turning this way and that. Wakefulness was on him. He heard the unresting wind, again risen, strumming over the cabin, he heard, like the far cries of children at play, the yapping of coyotes. Loneliness well-nigh more than he could bear beset him.

At last he fell asleep.

The slam of the door woke him, in broad daylight. Lacy was on his way to the stable. Jeff rolled out at once. The fire was going; he set about getting breakfast.

There was not much chance of bettering the fare. Jeff tried. He cleaned out the coffee pot and measured the coffee and water for a fresh brew. He sliced potatoes and set them cooking in water, instead of frying them. He toasted hard-tack and broiled bacon. It was all ready when Lacy came in.

"Come and get it," Jeff said.

"In just a minute," Lacy answered, too politely. He washed up, brushed his hair, and joined Jeff at table. The meal was eaten in an atmosphere of uneasy constraint.

When it was done, Lacy at once went back to the stable. Jeff cleaned up the dishes. It was not his job, station keepers were supposed to attend to the cooking and dishwashing.

Toward noon, Jeff caught the sound he had been longing for, the warning "eeh-yah!" of a rider coming in from Julesburg with the westbound mail. He jumped into his chaps, buckled on his gun belt, grabbed his coat and fur cap. Lacy brought out a pony. Everything was ready when the incoming courier drew rein on the crusty snow in front of the station.

"Hi, there!" he greeted.

"Hello!" Lacy and Jeff spoke as one. Then there was an instant's pause. It was Jeff who asked: "Riding for Bill? Anything happen to him?"

The youthful stranger's lean, clean-chiseled face showed no concern. "Bill quit," he said nonchalantly.

"How'd that come?"

"He quit, that's all. Froze his feet and frosted his face some, comin' down the other day. Kinda soured him on the job, I guess. Anyhow, he turned in his time, and caught the stage East. Swore he wuz a-goin' back to God's country— I dunno just what part. Believe he said something about heading for Ohio."

The rider had swung down. He stripped the mochila from his saddle and passed it to Jeff with an easy swing. From his beaver cap to his worn spurs, he looked hard, ready, competent.

"Been riding Express somewhere before, have you?" Lacy suggested.

"Yeah, west o' Salt Lake. Got tired o' bucking sand storms. I did figure I'd quit, myself, but I run into Cap'n Slade up at Rocky Ridge, 'n he talked me into taking a whirl at it on his division. I heard quite a bit about him out West, before ever I come back."

Jeff stepped into the leather. His pony, keyed high from confinement in the stable, sprang away with him. Its plunging hoofs threw a scurry of dry snow around Lacy and the dismounted courier.

As he shot away, Jeff lifted his hand in the usual farewell sign. Out of the tail of his eye he saw the high-flung fur-gauntleted hand of the new rider, and Lacy's half-hearted gesture.

JEFF was glad to head into the snowy solitude.

The overcast sky threatened storm. The wind blew bleak across the hills; dry snow was drifting over the old marks of the trail. Yet his spirits rose as the lonely miles slipped by under the willing feet of one pony after another. Dark came early, but the long night did not seem long. He got a cheery greeting at each relay station, and toward morning, as finely sifted snow was beginning to fall, swung down at Fort Laramie, cold, tired, hungry, unaccountably content.

"D'you reckon you could rassle a steak?" the stationman demanded, after the fresh rider had faded into the gray storm.

"Wow! Make it an inch thick!"

"Coming up! Got a quarter o' beef over 't the fort yesterday. Got some fresh light-bread, too. I'll fix you up right."

Jeff was well into his meal, faint light was showing in the windowpane, when his host remarked: "Been missing any horses down at the Springs?"

"No. Why?"

"Somebody made a getaway with two o' the best ones in the outfit up at Horseshoe, a couple o' nights ago. And Dead Timber station lost some, lately. Shouldn't wonder ef Pete Anderson was back at his old tricks again."

"Pete Anderson! I—I thought he went in more for bigger stuff—holdups and such." Jeff bent over and inspected his spur. He wondered whether his voice sounded funny or his face changed color. He was bound he wouldn't tell about Anderson's overnight stay at Mud Springs. The fewer the people who found out about that the better.

"He's in for anything that's mean, that fellow," declared the stationman, not noticing Jeff's embarrassment. "He'll steal horses when he don't have any good chanct to waylay a stage. This country'll be a sight better off when that hombre is rubbed out. He's killed four men, that I know of, in holdups. 'Twas him shot your brother, wasn't it?"

Jeff's face grew suddenly grim. "Yes."

"How'd your brother come out, anyhow?"

"He had quite a bad time of it, but he's about well now. Coming back onto the Express in the spring."

"Good for him. . . . You make a long arm and finish your breakfast, and turn in whenever you feel like it. I'm going out to the stable—one of the horses is off feed; I want to doctor him up."

126

The second day after that, about noon, the rider from the West showed up. "There's a letter in there come clear from China," he remarked, as he passed the mochila to Jeff. "Must be a heavy one, got a hundred and thirty-five dollars charges on it."

"Great guns! Who's it from?"

"Some kind of report from a British fleet to headquarters in London, that's what the fellow I got this mochiler from said."

Something of the thrill of his first Pony Express ride ran through Jeff as he fitted the mochila to his saddle—the magic of far places, the romance of the mail. An official communication for London from a British commander on the China coast! Pony Express charges on it more than a month's wage for a rider. This letter and all the other tissue-paper, silk-wrapped messages in the padlocked cantinas in his sole keeping along a hundred miles of empty, snow-blown trail.

An instant, this thrill; then again he saw the cold, hard saddle grind.

"I reckon, then, I better not lose that letter," he chaffed, as he set his foot in the stirrup.

"Not unless you're aiming to quit your job pronto," called the other rider.

"Just another ride," Jeff told himself. Riding had come to be his second nature. The steady "cluff-cluff" of hoofs in the snow, the faint creak of mochila against saddle, the rustle of chaps against icy leather, the sigh of the eternal wind across snowy, unfenced spaces—all had become part of him.

So he rode.

His keen, distance-trained gray eyes caught whatever moved along the silent way. Life was in these wintry wastes —a jack rabbit, white in winter fur, slipping through snow-tufted sagebrush; a hawk, wheeling, circling, swooping low, and banking in sharp turns; a pair of coyotes, one sitting on watch on the top of a butte, the other hunting in a coulee below. They noted the pastel colors of the snow, changing delicately in the shifting light.

The early dusk was made earlier by a veil of powdery, wind-driven snow from the north.

Ghostly darkness, the whirl dance of the storm, had been about him for long hours when he reached the last relay station. The snow, he knew, was deeper from here on to Mud Springs. His fresh pony plunged doggedly into the hindering drifts.

Jeff had often heard of Express riders sleeping in the saddle. Bill Johnson claimed to have slept more than half the way from Julesburg to the Springs one trip, coming awake at stations, trusting his ponies to keep the trail between relay points. Jeff, no matter how tired, had always stayed awake riding. But tonight darkness, weariness, and the joggle of the saddle set him nodding. He rode for a time with senses dulled, heedless of the snow rack, the cutting wind. He roused instantly when his pony stopped still.

The cloud-filtered moon now cast a faint half-light on the whirling snow. Jeff saw dark shapes ahead, spread out across the trail. They shifted, changed. A throaty snarl cut across the wind.

Lacy's words of long before came to Jeff: "Wolves? Well,

there's these coyotes, lots of them; they make plenty of noise, but it don't amount to anything. Then there's some gray wolves. They're big boys—trappers call 'em buffalo wolves, because they hang around big herds. They can hamstring a buffalo or a horse quicker than you can say Jack Robinson. But they don't usually tackle a man—unless they're mighty hungry."

Jeff pulled his Colt and aimed at the shifting pack. The hammer clicked on a bad cap. He pressed the trigger again, but the cylinder stuck. He fumbled with it in the darkness, but could not make it turn.

He yelled, and spurred his pony. The wolves drew off to both sides of the trail as the trembling, snorting pony advanced, then closed in behind. Jeff saw them following. The pony went into a frantic gallop. He let it have free rein. Behind, dark on the snow, the snarling pack pressed on. The pony struck a wind-swept stretch of shallow snow and burst into a run.

Smash! The pony went down. It rolled over, lay in a heap. Jeff lit free. He jumped up, grabbed the rein as the pony got falteringly to its feet. The wolves circled warily.

Jeff did not try to mount. One of the pony's forelegs did not look right. When he got his matches and struck a light he saw it dangled sickeningly. While the yellow eyes of the wolves ringed him, he struck match after match, and finally loosened the jammed revolver cylinder.

He lifted off the mochila. Then he untied the latigos and pulled off the saddle. He struck two more matches and examined the dangling leg. Then he set his teeth, held the revolver behind the pony's ear, and fired. The pony slumped in its tracks, quivered, and lay still.

Jeff slung the mochila over his arm, picked up the saddle, and trudged ahead, with his revolver, a poor weapon against buffalo wolves, ready in case they rushed him. The pack snarled and fought over the pony.

He laid the saddle down about fifty yards from the feasting wolves, and plodded on carrying the mochila. The going soon got bad. The trail marks were nearly filled with drifted snow. The flopping mochila hindered him, he slipped and floundered with his high-heeled boots. Noises of the pack came to him on the wind long after darkness hid the blot on the snow behind.

The drifts got deeper. The powdery swirl made it hard to breathe. He shook himself and kept going. The noise of the wolves died away. The hostile wind, the numbing cold, the hindering snow dogged him.

On, on. The mochila got heavier every minute. He stopped and rested a little, plunged ahead. The wind rose higher; the snow whirled more fiercely. He set his teeth and plodded on.

His strength was worn low when, in the whirl dance of the storm, he dimly saw a low pine tree. Then he knew he was on the trail. The station was a mile ahead.

He was too near winded to yell. He plodded up to the snow-banked little cabin and beat on the door with fists and feet.

"Who's there?" Lacy called.

"It's me, Jeff! Let me in!"

He heard a thump and a rattle, then his partner swung

the door back. The lantern he held up shone blindingly in Jeff's eyes. "What's the matter, Jeff?"

"Tiptop stepped in a hole and broke his leg. I had to shoot him. Buffalo wolves were after us."

Jeff dropped the mochila on the floor and sat down wearily. The relay rider threw off his blanket and sat up alertly in his bunk. Without a word or a lost motion he drew on his trousers, his boots, buckled on his gun belt. Lacy hurried out to the stable and came back with a pony. The courier, fur-capped and ready, caught up the mochila and slipped out. A farewell yell, a wave of the lantern, and the mail went on into the whirling storm.

Lacy came back in and barred the door. Jeff stood up and spread his hands above the stove. Danger, stress, the hard need of shooting his pony had wrought him up. His mind, keyed high, was strangely alert. He knew, in a wordless way he did not understand, yet was sure of, that Lacy was glad to have him back again. The trouble between them was over. A warm and friendly feeling filled the room.

Lacy set the lantern on the table and came over to the stove. There was a space of silence, intimate and grateful. The wind swooping over the roof, the beating snow, the black night, made the cabin a homelike place.

"Hungry?" Lacy asked.

"Not so very."

"Well, you better have something." Lacy turned to the shelves along the wall. "Got some potatoes left. I'll warm 'em up. And a piece of ham. Oh, yes, here's something else." He set a small paper sack on the table in the yellow light. "Help yourself while I get this stuff ready."

131

Jeff looked into the sack. He drew out a striped stick of candy. "Where'd you get hold of this, Jack?"

"Tom brought it up from Julesburg. I saved it for you."

"Tom?"

"Yep—that new rider. Tom Neal's his name."

"First candy I've seen for quite a spell," Jeff commented, as he munched.

"Same here. Tom brought up a fresh paper too."

"Where is it?"

Lacy brought it out, and Jeff scanned it as he ate. "Did you see this?" he demanded, presently.

"What?"

"Some kind of trouble down in South Carolina—Charleston. Says the forts there fired on a government steamer, the *Star of the West*. Drove her away."

"I didn't see that. Read it."

"It's written by a newspaperman on the *Star of the West*, starts telling about coming into the harbor," Jeff explained, and read:

"Now, about half-past six o'clock, we see the lighthouse, and now, too, we discover that the mysterious light was that of a steamer on our right. Now the steamer is burning red and blue lights, and now she sends up rockets. There is no mistaking her movements; she is giving the alarm signal to Fort Moultrie.

"On we go—the soldiers are below with loaded muskets, and the officers are ready to give the word if there is anything to do. Now we discover a red Palmetto flag at our left, on Morris Island.

"It is now a quarter past seven, and we are about two miles from Forts Sumter and Moultrie, which are equidistant from us, and suddenly whiz-z! comes a ricochet shot from Morris Island. It plunges into the water and skips along, but falls short of our steamer. The line of fire was forward of our bows, and was of course an invitation to stop. But the captain pays no attention except to run up the stars and stripes at the masthead.

"Another moment and *bang* goes a heavy cannon from the same masked battery. The ball strikes our ship in the fore chains about two feet above the water. A seaman was holding the lead to take soundings and the ball struck directly under his feet. The ball, fortunately, was too far spent to go through the side of our vessel, although it left an honorable scar. A moment longer and we shall be in range of three batteries.

" 'Helm out of port!' shouts the captain, and the *Star of the West* is turned about. We turn without accident and steam away, with the stars and stripes still floating and the batteries still playing upon us by way of a parting salute."

"What was all the fuss about, anyhow?" Lacy asked.

"I don't know." Jeff was glancing through the paper as he spoke. "But it seems this *Star of the West* was going down there with supplies for Fort Sumter, and the Charleston authorities wouldn't let her land. . . . Here's something queer, Jack. It says South Carolina, Mississippi, Florida, Alabama, and Georgia have seceded. What's that mean?"

"Reckon it means they're going to go on their own hook from now on," Lacy replied, carelessly.

"And not be part of the United States anymore? How can they do that? It'll be mighty bad if this country goes to splitting up!"

"Oh, they'll manage to keep house, one way or another. I don't care much what they do, just so old Virginia doesn't get mixed up in any trouble. She's *my* state. . . . What say we turn in? Somebody'll have to ride back up the trail in the morning and get that saddle and bridle, if they're not torn to pieces."

"I'll tend to it."

"Better let me go. Do me good to get out. And we'll have to send a report to Slade, so he can send up another horse."

Jeff lounged idly against a counter in the sutler's store at Fort Laramie. A third day of inaction hung heavy on him. The mail from the West was two days overdue. The sight of the flag on the staff at the parade ground gave him an idea; he approached the storekeeper.

Midafternoon of the next day, chilled to the bone, his face raked red by wind, Jeff rode up to the snow-banked Mud Springs station. He yelled as he neared, a shrill yell across the cutting air.

No one showed. He yelled again; Lacy came through the doorway as he slid stiffly out of the saddle.

"Make it all right, did you?" Lacy asked.

"Reckon so." Jeff rubbed his frost-stiffened cheeks. "Where's Tom?"

"In there. Sick. Can't hold his head up."

A wordless pause. "Well, I'll go in and thaw out a little," Jeff said, then.

"Sure."

Lacy caught up the rein, led Jeff's frost-white pony around to the stable. Jeff walked into the snug warmth of the station. He hovered over the stove. Stinging pains shot through his cheeks as he stood warming; he knew he had just missed freezing his face.

"How is it, out?" Tom Neal's voice came low from a bunk.

"Cold. Drifting quite a bit."

"Sorry I'm all in. Just let that thing lay till morning." His eyes flicked the mochila Jeff had laid on the floor. I'll be all right then; I'll take it on."

Lacy came stamping and puffing in from the stable. A breath of bitter air swept in with him. He walked over to the stove and stood beside Jeff. The stovepipe rattled as the wind swept across the sod roof.

The low-slanting sun broke for an instant through the snow rack and sent a bright shaft through the little window. Full in the sudden glow lay the mochila. Jeff swung his gaze to look at it.

It gleamed with strange richness in the small, rough room. Brown it was, battered, weathered, scarred, but worn smooth in the middle by the chaps of riders who had brought it through snow-hung passes of the Sierras and across desolate Humboldt Sink and the still more forbidding wastes of the great white desert beyond Salt Lake.

Those regions were only names to Jeff, but he knew the mountain country beyond Fort Laramie, from talk with other riders. Over the lonely fifty-five mile stretch from Fort Bridger to Green River Crossing it had come, along Big Sandy, across the continental divide by way of South Pass, past Burnt Ranch, past Ice Slough station, over the three treacherous crossings of the Sweetwater, through Devil's Gate, past Independence Rock, Sweetwater station, Willow Springs, Platte Bridge, Deer Creek, Labonte Creek, Dead Timber, Cottonwood and Horseshoe, and so into Laramie. Four hundred hard miles from Fort Bridger to Laramie, but that was only one-fifth of the Pony Express trail! This far the picked riders of the border had brought this battered pouch—vital tie between East and West halves of an empire.

Now the sunlight lay along the dirt floor like a hand pointing. Like it had lain the day Chet took the Express rider's oath. Chet—who well-nigh had given his life for the mail.

Jeff paced back and forth in the narrow room, the rustle of his wolfskin chaps, the tinkle of his spur, sounded in the silence. "Get me a horse," he said, turning on Lacy. "I'll get this into Julesburg." His glance again touched the mochila, dull brown now, as swirling snow hid the cold sunlight.

"You've had a hard trip already, it's getting colder, too. Do you think you can—"

"Hell, yes!"

Lacy shrugged his shoulders. He glanced at the bunk where Neal lay, at the waiting mochila with its padlocked compartments, and again at Jeff. Then he turned up his coat collar, pulled down his cap, drew on his gloves. The plank door, hard-yanked against the snowy blast, thudded shut behind him as he went out to the stable.

When Jeff got back to Mud Springs, three days later, Neal and Lacy were standing outside the station to greet him. A fresh pony stood ready. The weather had turned mild and cloudy; the wind was stilled.

"How'd you make it?" they demanded.

"All right." Jeff restrained an impulse to touch his cheeks, sore from frost bite. "How you feeling, Tom?"

"Ready for business," Neal grinned, self-consciously. "That spell t'other day was the second time in my life I ever had the cramps. Don't know what brought 'em on. I'll take this on to Laramie, Jeff, and sort o' even things up."

"Unh-uh! I'm all set and raring to go. I know the trail up there like a book." Jeff had changed the mochila as he talked.

"You don't need to go this time." Neal stepped close, his face, still pale and drawn, was earnest. "You're not the only hombre that knows the trail."

"You might get lost." Jeff grinned with sure good-humor as he swung into the saddle. He forgot the pain of his cracked lips. The easy grace of his upflung arm made his farewell gesture knightly.

He was two days late getting back to the Springs. Lacy and Neal had to have their say. "Made up your mind to come, finally, did you? We 'lowed the wolves'd made a clean job of it this time, or else the superintendent had maybe made up a new easy schedule for you. Or maybe you like the grub up at Laramie better?"

Jeff swung the icy mochila over to Tom. "Needn't blame me," he returned, easily. "I held up my end. Trouble was out West—slides in the Sierras, and snow and wind from Bridger to the Sweetwater."

Tom Neal forced the mochila into place over his saddle with a hard jerk, and mounted. "I'm for a short life, and an easy one, that's why I'm on the Pony Express." With this parting quip, he swung south into the drifted Julesburg trail.

Lacy took Jeff's pony. Jeff passed into the dusky warmth

of the cabin. He remembered, now, what he had been carrying in an inner pocket ever since his previous trip down from Fort Laramie.

Lacy, when he came stamping in from his chores, did not see the bit of color that stirred overhead as a puff of cold air swept in. The lantern was burning, but its narrow radiance fell on the table. Then, as he crossed the room, he noticed something just above his head. "What's that?" he exclaimed.

Jeff held the lantern up.

From a cord tied to the low roof-poles hung a small flag. The lantern light lit up the red and white stripes, the blue canton bearing thirty-three stars.

"Where'd you get that thing?" Lacy demanded.

"Up at the Fort. I thought it would look good here in the station."

Lacy hesitated. He looked at Jeff rather than at the flag. His concern in that moment was plainly for his partner's good will, not for an ensign.

"It's all right, I suppose, if you want it," he said, his tone carefully casual.

Jeff set the lantern back on the table. "I'm hungry as a bear tonight," he said, with a quick grin. He had no words for the faint uneasiness that came to him as he looked again at the flag, dimly outlined now in the half-light.

THE days were growing longer. A mild wind breathed over the snow, the southern slopes of the hills turned suddenly brown and bare.

"Want me to toss a target for you?" Lacy asked, as he watched Jeff loading the Smith and Wesson twenty-two revolver Slade had sent him.

"Yeah, wish you would. Pick out a good big one. I haven't had any practice for a month."

They went out in front of the station, where the trampled gravelly ground was beginning to dry under the sun and wind. Lacy picked up a slab from the wood pile. Jeff slid the revolver carefully into his gun belt. "All right," he called.

Lacy heaved the chunk high into the air. Jeff's hand flashed to his holster. The gun cracked. Bits of bark flew from the target.

"Got it!" Lucy exclaimed, approvingly.

Half an hour later, the ground where Jeff stood was littered with empty cartridges. Lacy, not needed and tired of looking on, had gone to the stable. Jeff was tossing up a cedar knot three or four inches in diameter, drawing his gun after making the toss. He was still at it when Lacy sauntered back.

"How're you making it?"

"Hit it twice out of three, just now. I'm going to quit on that, for today."

"You better quit. You don't want to get to be a better shot than Slade is," Lacy jested.

"No chance. But I'm going to practice some every day, when it gets a little warmer."

That night the wind shifted and roared angrily over the stanch little cabin. The slushy snow in the buffalo wallows turned to solid ice.

The first of March, 1861. The fourth of March was the day for which the nation waited.

While Tom Neal set up the checkermen for a new game, Lacy reached over and threw more wood into the stove. Then, from habit rather than expectation, he crossed to the window and glanced south. His gaze instantly narrowed.

"Somebody's coming!" he exclaimed. "I believe it's Slade!" He snatched his cap and went out. Tom watched from the doorway as the rider came up.

140

"Good morning, Captain," they greeted.

"Good morning. How's everything?"

"All right, sir," Lacy responded. "Harlowe is probably halfway to Laramie with the mail, by this time. Won't you come in a while, sir?"

"Not this time, thanks. Headquarters has ordered a fast run with President Lincoln's inaugural address. Fort Kearny will get it over the wire on the afternoon of March fourth. A rider will start from there with it as soon as it gets in. California is very anxious to get this quickly. Tell Harlowe to push his horses to the limit, regardless of weather or anything else. That goes for you, too, Neal. Understand?"

"Yes, sir," they both responded. "I'll tell Jeff to hammer it through," Lacy added.

Slade's eyes, blue now, impassive, turned ahead to the Laramie trail; he spurred his sharp-shod horse across the crunching, icy crusts.

"At length we greet the long-expected day. Abraham Lincoln and Hannibal Hamlin, will, ere night, be inaugurated President and Vice-President of the United States for the ensuing four years. . . .

"We bespeak for our new rulers the generous confidence of the American people. Never before have men assumed responsibility under such fearful disadvantages. A bankrupt Treasury, a disorganized Army, ruined Finances, seven revolted States, with others strongly sympathizing and prepared on the least pretext to make common cause with them, and hundreds of thousands, even in the Free States, waiting and hoping to see them stumble and fall—such are the fearful odds which Mr. Lincoln and his associates are summoned to confront at the threshold of their official career." [12]

A bleak wind swept across the Platte Valley on the late afternoon of March 4, 1861. The flag was being lowered from the tall staff on the Fort Kearny parade ground, a pastel sunset was glowing palely, as the Pony Express station-man crunched across the snow and walked into Mose Sydenham's post office, store, and telegraph office. The narrow room was full of men. In a railed-off corner Ellsworth, the operator, sat at his key. He had a sheaf of penciled tissue-paper sheets on the table in front of him. The sounder was quiet.

"How's it coming, Ellsworth?" demanded the Pony Express man.

"Got part of it, about half, Omaha says. They'll start sending again in a minute. Might be half an hour yet before it's all in."

"All right. I'll go back and get things lined up."

His boot heels sounded on the puncheon floor as he pushed out. When he came back, darkness was closing in. With him came a sun-bronzed, slender lad wearing buckskin and a fur cap, leading a rangy pony. The mochila of the Express was over its saddle. They tied the pony to a post and went in, threading their way to Ellsworth's table. The sounder was clicking steadily now; Ellsworth, by the light of a small oil lamp, wrote on sheet after sheet of flimsy. The wire thrummed outside; the fire crackled in the stove. There was no other sound save the rustle of paper under Ellsworth's pencil.

He wrote mechanically, yet as the message drew to its close he became aware of high and brooding beauty in the words he set down:

"In your hands, my dissatisfied fellow countrymen, and not in mine, is the momentous issue of civil war. The government will not assail you. You can have no conflict without being yourselves the aggressors. You have no oath registered in heaven to destroy the government, while I shall have the most solemn one to preserve, protect and defend it.

"I am loath to close. We are not enemies but friends. Though passion may have strained, it must not break our bonds of affection. The mystic chords of memory stretching from every battle-field and patriot grave, to every living heart and hearthstone all over this broad land, will yet swell the chorus of the Union when again touched, as surely they will be, by the better angels of our nature."

"That's all," clicked the Omaha operator.

Ellsworth picked up his sheets and hastily folded them into an envelope. "Here is it," he said.

The waiting Express man took it, wheeled, and strode to the door. The rider kept step with him.

"You know what to do, Joe," the man said, as he crammed the envelope into a cantina and snapped the brass padlock.

"You bet." The rider swung up. No ribbons on his buck-skin jacket, none on the pony's bridle, no cheers from the crowd around the doorway, though hands were flung up in farewell. He crouched over the pony's withers, there was a crunching of hoofs, a skurry of broken crust, and the special mail shot away into the icy darkness.

Jeff, restless in his bunk, heard a distant whoop and instantly rolled out. He lit the lantern and shook Lacy before he stamped into his boots. "Hustle!" he exclaimed, "Tom's coming!"

A forlorn band of pale yellow showed in the eastern sky

143

when they opened the door. Neal rode up a moment later, got out of the saddle stiffly, and jerked savagely at the mochila. "Colder than blue blazes!" he snapped. "You all set?"

"In a second," Jeff assured him. "Go on inside. Jack's after my pony"

Neal stood hardily where he was. A bobbing lantern showed yellow; Lacy led a pony up through the crusted snow.

"What you got on its legs?" Neal demanded.

"We tied on some old sacks last night," Jeff explained. "Probably be some bad crust, after that thaw. I thought—"

"Huh! Lot o' good that'll do," Neal scoffed. Stepping back into semidarkness, he ran a hand down over his pony's fetlocks, then slyly wiped something warm and wet from his fingers. "Mebbe, though, if they stay on, they might help a little," he conceded.

"They sure won't do any harm," Jeff said, cheerfully. "So long, fellows." Then the icy snow popped under his horse's feet and he was gone.

" 'Nother one o' them stunt trips," Neal grumbled, as he hovered over the stove. Lacy, back from the stable, put in more wood. The stove began to hum. Lacy poked around among his dishes in the lantern light, he sliced bacon into the skillet. The frosted windowpane now showed white.

"Yeah," he agreed. "They're not liable to break any records this time."

"Sure not. March is the worst time o' the whole year. Boy, I'll bet she's tough up along the Sweetwater now, and through South Pass!"

144

"Wasn't any picnic out of Julesburg, was it? Move that coffee back a little, will you."

"No." Neal shoved the pot over to the edge of the stove. "Say! I forgot to tell you about the holdup!"

"Whereabouts?"

"Eastbound stage from Denver about fifty miles below Julesburg. Two fellows stuck it up—shot the driver in the arm and got away with three thousand dollars' worth of dust. The stage got to Julesburg a couple of hours before I left."

"What'd they do about it?"

"Started a posse out after 'em. Slade was in it."

"That wasn't on his division."

"That don't make any difference to him. They won't have much chance to do anything, though. It was snowing and blowing down there—tracks would be covered up in five minutes, the driver said."

"Any idea who the fellows were?"

"Driver said they wore masks, but he was pretty sure one of 'em was Anderson."

"Hm." Lacy set the skilletful of bacon on the glowing stove. His mind swung to the thing they had been talking about. "What was the best run the Pony Express ever made, Tom?"

"That election special last fall. Three or four hours under seven days, Kearny to Fort Churchill. *That* was moving right along. Look at us now—supposed to get through in twelve days on the winter schedule, and we're taking from fourteen to sixteen, nearly every trip."

"Well, as long as your pay goes on, what d'you care?" Lacy turned the strips of bacon. "I'll have this stuff ready now in a jiffy, Tom, and after you get filled up you can roll in and snooze all day, if you feel like it."

Jeff found the going harder than he expected. The trail was icy. Beyond the first relay station he struck fresh snow; it got deeper as he fought his way toward Fort Laramie.

The slow day wore away, he pressed on in the darkness and the muffling snow. His last pony was tired out; he himself was numb and dizzy when, at midnight, he rode up to the Laramie station. The waiting rider grinned a welcome; he stood slim, confident, ready.

"Looks like you had a tough trip," he said. "I figure it'll get no better fast, up in the hills. If they want a quick run, they'd better pick the good old summertime for it."

His upflung hand showed in the lantern's dim aureole, then he was gone into the night and the cold.

Days of dull routine followed, lengthening days, the sun dazzlingly bright on the snow, the snow suddenly melting under a warm wind. Nile-green tints on southern slopes of the winter-starved prairie. Word coming back from the west end, passed from rider to rider along with an eastbound mochila, that the Express with the inaugural address got to Fort Churchill March 17, thirteen days out of Kearny, after a heart-breaking fight against mountain snows and desert storms. Thirteen days—a record, not of time, but of nerve and pluck.

XII   AMBUSHED

THE wet, living smell of spring was in the air. The wind blew chill; patches of flinty snow still clung in hillside pockets, but new grass was coming green under last year's dull brown. The sun was warm as Jeff, eastbound, pulled up about noon at the last relay station on the Laramie—Mud Springs run.

The waiting stationman had a firm grip on the bridle of a slim, black horse.

"What you got there?" Jeff demanded.

"This is a new un. They just brought him up yesterday. Got him off'n a half-breed scout that used to carry dispatches back and forth from Laramie to Kearny, so I reckon he knows the trail. He looks fast, and acts tricky. The other stuff here ain't in any kinda shape. Flint ain't got over that sprain; Rex is clean off his feed, and Smoke is just naturally played out."

"This looks like a good one to me."

"Yep, Star's the best I've seen for a while. Whoa, boy; steady, now." He tightened his hold on the bit as Jeff eased the mochila onto the side-stepping black.

"How's things up the line, Jeff?"

"Quiet as ever."

"See any Indians?"

"Haven't seen an Indian for so long I most forget what they look like."

"Well, I been kinda keepin' my eye peeled, specially since the snow went off. Some o' these Sioux from up north is liable to be out to see what they can find. They've been laying low all winter, seems like, and they're probably full of devilment."

"Shouldn't wonder. But I usually figure after I get through that rough country up around Scott's Bluff there's not much more chance of running into anything."

Everything was ready. Jeff mounted, the man let go Star's head, and the nervous black swung down the trail, snorting, shying, thrusting at the bit. Jeff held him in, talked to him, and by and by the horse settled into a smooth, flowing gallop.

Jeff rode with skilled instinct, but his conscious mind was not on his horsemanship. He was thinking of Chet, who had written that he was about ready to start West. Jeff had spoken to Slade about a place for him; Slade had suggested

148

that Chet apply to the superintendent of the Fort Kearny division for a place before coming on out to Julesburg. Now that winter was over riders were sticking closer to their jobs. It would be great to have Chet back anywhere on the Express, Jeff felt, though of course he'd like most of all to have him on the Julesburg division.

A heady elation ran now in Jeff's thoughts, mingled with a faintly disturbing and elusive sense of unguessed danger. He thought again of Pete Anderson, whose slippery daring was making him almost a legendary figure. The posse hunting Anderson after the stage holdup had come back jaded and empty-handed. Jeff thought of what Slade had once told him, and, as he rode, loosened his Colt in its holster.

A few miles out from the station the trail ran through a deep coulee, where patches of flinty snow lay on the steep banks. Jeff held Star to an easy gallop. The horse started nervously, shying first to one side, then to the other. Jeff, becoming alert, scanned the coulee sides, sloping up to hide from sight the prairie on either side. He saw nothing out of the way. He urged Star on; they came near the further end of the ravine.

Whir-r! An arrow shot past. He felt the wind of it against his cheek! It stuck with quivering shaft in the bank beside the trail.

At this signal, a shower of arrows flew down from the brows of the coulee. Some fell short, some shot overhead.

Jeff flattened himself along Star's withers. He yelled; the black leaped forward. He jerked his Colt from its holster. They flashed out of the coulee.

Jeff, glancing back, saw a dozen Indians scrambling onto

ponies and starting after him, yelling. His Colt barked twice. Star leveled out in great bounds. Gravel and clots of grass sprayed out behind his thudding hoofs.

The shrill Indian war whoop rang. More arrows flew by. Crouching still lower, Jeff.glanced back again.

Star, going like a prairie wind, was moving away from the main bunch. Two Indians, only, had mounts that could match the black horse's speed. Jeff saw these two braves, one on a bright bay, one on a roan, drawing ahead of the yelling group. He saw the red and yellow paint on their hawklike faces, saw the fluttering feathers of their bonnets, saw them drawing their bows. He fired twice more. He could not hold the gun steady against the bounding jerks of his horse; he was surprised to see one of the ponies in the main bunch stumble and fall. Arrows zipped past him.

He yelled, crouching along Star's neck. The flying black stretched out in a gallant burst of speed. The pursuing roan could not keep up the pace, it faded back into the main bunch. The bay held on. Some potent strain of wild blood was in its speed. It could not gain on Star, but momently it kept its place. Jeff saw the lean, painted savage again drawing his bow. He fired his revolver without sure aim, he bent low in the saddle, he tried to swerve. A blasting pain ran through him. He almost fell.

Now Star's speed was drawing them away from even the Indian on the bright bay. Jeff, gasping, pulling leather, kept his seat. He watched a red stain spreading down his buck-skin jacket. A blotch of red showed on the brown mochila. He grew faint. . . .

Star, affrighted, unchecked, was running now like a wild thing.

Lacy and Tom Neal, on the sunny side of the station, were throwing hunting knives at a piece of paper tacked on the cabin wall. A fresh pony, saddled and bridled, was tied at the door of the stable. The Pony Express, now spring had come, was running closer to schedule; they figured Jeff would likely show up about midafternoon.

Lacy hit the target fairly with a lucky throw. Then, from long habit, he glanced northward along the trail.

Even as he glanced, a black horse bobbed into sight half a mile away. It dropped from sight as the trail dipped, then showed again, closer and coming on.

"There he comes," Lacy said. He turned to go to the stable. Neal, putting up his knife, started to get his gun belt. Lacy looked again. "Look yonder, Tom!" he exclaimed.

They both looked. The black horse was only a quarter of a mile away; their distance-trained eyes saw something was not right. As it galloped its head time and again jerked sharply downward. A trailing bridle rein, stepped on, would do that. Something was the matter with the rider. He slumped in the saddle, like a thing flung loosely onto the horse's back. "Like a sack o' oats," was Neal's way of telling it, afterward. For all that, there he was, in his place. But Lacy, instead of going to fetch the fresh pony, watched wonderingly that which now was coming into the station. Coming in on time.

Useless to go to meet them, for the foam-spattered black held its dogged gallop, despite the harsh jerking of the

151

trailing rein. Yet, as it came in, both watchers ran forward. They were alongside before it stopped, their hands checking it and holding the swaying lad in the saddle.

"What's the matter, Jeff?" they begged, huskily.

Jeff tried to grin. He spoke through pale lips, his low voice matter-of-fact: "Indians. Ambushed me in Lone Coulee."

Lacy and Neal eased him out of the saddle, carried him into the cabin, laid him in a bunk. They pulled off the torn buckskin jacket, the calico shirt. Jeff made no sound. Lacy drew a long breath that was almost a sob. Neal let out a savage malediction. "Git some water," he directed, then.

Lacy brought a bucket. Silently, with rough tenderness, they washed away some of the blood. Neal spoke briskly: "Boy, you're not dead yet, by a long ways! That nipped you along the back and here on your arm. It sure bled plenty—mebbe that's a good thing."

Lacy tore up an old shirt. They bandaged the wounds, then withdrew just outside the open door. As from a great distance, faintly, Jeff heard their voices. Lacy's first:

"That don't look good to me. He ought to have a doctor—"

"Doctor, hell! You know there ain't a sawbones this side o' Laramie! It's up to us. If it don't bleed too much—"

"We better look at it again."

They came to the bunk. Neal whistled softly as the soaked bandage was unwound from Jeff's arm. "Here," he said, sharply, "let's have some more of that shirt, a good stout piece." He wound it above the gash, and twisted it tight with a short stick. So, holding this in place, they stanched the bleeding.

And when this was done, there remained the ever-present care of every Pony Express rider and stationman. The mail!

"Reckon you can handle him now?" Neal asked.

"Yes, I reckon so."

"You don't figure that bunch of Indians'll bother the station, do you?"

"Unh-uh, they'll stay in the clear and not take any chances. You better be moving. Say, Tom——"

"Yeah?"

"Hunt around some in Julesburg and see if you can't fetch up something for him next trip."

"Like what?"

"Why, anything that'll help him. Some—some salve, maybe, or—hell! There ain't a blasted thing here for a sick man, you know that. Fetch up some rags for bandages, for one thing." Lacy's restless fingers had been working in his trousers pocket; he held out a yellow coin.

Neal seemed not to see the money. "Sure, I'll look around," he said. "Keep it," he added, as Lacy would have pressed the coin upon him. "Well, if you think you'll be all right with him, I better hit the grit."

He went out and got the fresh pony, while Lacy stood beside Jeff's bunk. He wet a piece of old sack, wiped the dried blood from the mochila, and changed it over from the tired and docile black to the other saddle.

Lacy crossed to the doorway. "I reckon he'll be all right," he said, doubtfully.

"Sure. But watch him—don't let that get started again."
He swung into the saddle. "I'll tell Slade, Jack."

"All right."

Only an hour late, the Pony Express took the eastward trail.

XIII   THE MAIL KEEPS MOVING

LACY, the third morning thereafter, stood in front of the station and waved his hat as Tom Neal rode toward him through spring sunshine. He grinned as Tom came closer.

"How's he making it?" the rider called.

"He's on the mend, now."

At this instant Jeff showed in the doorway, his face pale and drawn, his hair rumpled.

"Hi, chief!" Neal greeted. "Say, Jack, I believe he looks better'n you do, at that. Let's see—my memory's failing—which one of you fellows was it stopped an arrow, anyhow?"

They both grinned. Neal swung down. He dumped a blanket roll in front of them. "A little stuff for you, Jeff. How you feeling?"

"Fine and dandy."

"Well, let me have a pony, Jack," Neal went on, briskly. "I'm going through to Laramie. They'll have an extra man up here in a day or two, I reckon, to fill in."

"Got one all ready." Lacy hurried to the stable.

Neal picked up the blanket roll and carried it to Jeff, who had walked unsteadily back into the station and sat down. "Julesburg ain't St. Joe nor St. Louis, you know, Jeff," he said, nonchalantly. "Not much down there. But maybe some o' this might come in handy."

A bright square of sunshine from the doorway fell on a tumbled array of packages as he unrolled the blanket.

"What's all this, Tom?"

"I gotta go." Neal strode out as the fresh pony's hoofs grated in the gravel. "Take care of yourself." He was off in a hard gallop.

Jeff and Lacy opened the packages. Four cans of condensed milk, half a dozen lemons, a tiny jar labeled "Doctor Wakefield's Golden Ointment," a pair of white pillow slips, old but clean, a suit of underwear, a calico shirt.

"Well, by the great horn spoon!" Lacy exclaimed. "Where do you reckon he rounded up all this?"

"Lemons!" Jeff's voice was husky. "Last time I saw a lemon was at a Fourth of July celebration—back home." The sight of the tropic fruit, unlooked for, exotic in the bare cabin; still more, the kindness that had brought it there, did that to Jeff which not loneliness nor hard living nor Indian arrow had done. Something bright came up in his eyes, spilled down his cheeks. He turned his head quickly; he got up and walked around the stove, winking hard. He cleared his throat before he spoke. "What say we have some lemonade, Jack?"

"You bet your boots." Lacy sprang to his feet. "I'll rustle some fresh water. Maybe you'd like to cut 'em up. There's a bowl on the table we can make it in."

They were sipping lemonade—Jeff would not drink it alone, when he looked straight at his partner. "I didn't get what Tom was driving at," he said, "joshing about not knowing which one of us got hurt, but now I see you do look kind of played out. I reckon I've been a lot of bother."

"You wasn't any special bother. Not to speak of."

"One day, there, I don't remember about. Was I out of my head, do you reckon?"

"Well, you might have been, a little, at that. You kept talking a lot of stuff—mostly about your brother."

A faraway look came into Jeff's eyes. His refilled glass of lemonade stood untouched till Lacy rallied him.

The extra rider came up from Julesburg with Neal and the mail a couple of days later—a man almost thirty, lean, leather-hard, taciturn. He took the mochila on to Laramie. Jeff watched him impatiently, almost jealously. "I believe I can swing it again myself next trip," he suggested to Neal, as the substitute was riding off and Lacy was putting up Tom's pony.

"You lay low for a while. 'Tain't healthy to crowd your luck."

Jeff settled down, warned by pain and weakness more than by Tom's advice.

He was loafing in the April sunshine one forenoon a few days later, his back against the log wall of the station.

Lacy and Neal were out at the stable. His first impulse was to call them when he saw, half a mile away, a rider coming up the Julesburg trail. Not reason, but quick feeling, kept him silent. Instinct told him, before his keen eyes were sure, that he wanted to welcome this comer all by himself.

He got up and walked out a few steps, and so waited till the other rode up. His thin face went pale. So did the tanned face of the rider. Their hands met and clung in a hard grip.

"Chet!"

"Jeff!"

"I been wishing you'd show up."

"How're you making it? I heard you got hurt."

"Oh, I'm all right again—just about." Jeff shrugged his shoulders ever so slightly, and winced. "They got a fellow in here riding for me, but I'm going to go myself about the next trip. How're you? When did you come out? Got a place? Did you see Slade?"

Chet grinned happily. He swung down; his steady gray eyes met Jeff's squarely. "You want to be careful," he said, protectingly. "Don't rush things. It takes time for a fellow to get back in shape after he's been laid out. I got a job on the Kearny division, riding between Cottonwood and Alkali Lake. Slade told me I better take it, he didn't have anything up here. He told me you're one of his best riders, old man."

Jeff thrilled. He tried to speak carelessly. "Come on in and see our layout. I'll tie your horse here. The fellows'll be in pretty soon, then we'll put him up."

That day made up to Jeff for some of his lonely days. How admiringly his eyes followed this big brother—become as hard and brown and strong as ever. There was plenty to talk about. Lacy and Neal wanted to know about one matter particularly. But Chet insisted there was nothing in his encounter with Pete Anderson worth the telling.

"It was all over in a second," he declared. "Two fellows rode up in front of me, one rainy night, and ordered me off my horse. I pulled my gun and gave my horse the spur. Just then the lightning flashed, and one of the fellows fired. He was tall, slim, kind of sharp-faced. I cut loose with my gun, but his bullet shook me up so it spoiled my aim. I beat it on down the trail and got away from them."

"Did they follow you?" Neal asked.

"Not very far."

"Was that a good ways out from any station?"

"Couple of miles, maybe."

"Anderson stayed overnight here with us once, since that," Lacy averred, meddlesomely.

Jeff reddened and shifted uncomfortably in his seat. Chet's gaze narrowed. "How was that?" he asked.

Lacy related the episode. "Needn't say anything about it, Chet," he added. "We wouldn't care to have Slade find it out."

Tom Neal switched the talk to the subject of guns and marksmanship. Lacy presently attempted to make up for his untactfulness. "Jeff is getting to be about as handy with a gun as any fellow I know of," he remarked. "I tell him if he don't let up on practicing so much he'll get to be bet-ter'n Slade himself."

Chet looked at his brother with approving interest. "Let's see what you can do," he suggested.

Jeff had never felt less like showing off. He hung back. That made them insist the more.

Slowly, then, he put on his gun belt. Lacy stood opposite him, and at his word tossed up a block of wood. Jeff drew, fired, missed. On his second trial, he missed again. His wound throbbed, he wiped his forehead, he knew unhappily that his face was flushed.

Anger mounted in him. He resented the watchful eyes around him, resented Lacy's telling about his sorry encounter with Anderson, resented his wound. His nerves tightened; he mastered himself.

"That's too big a chunk," he said, forcing a grin. "Pick out a little one, Jack."

Lacy looked around, found a smaller block, tossed it into the air.

Long training of hand and eye flashed into focus for Jeff in that instant. The watchers saw only a blur in the movement with which he drew; the gun cracked; the block split in midair.

"Good boy!" came the chorus.

"Toss another one," Jeff said.

He hit the second fairly, replaced his Smith and Wesson in his holster, and turned away. "Believe I'll quit on that."

Something of respect and admiration was in the glances Neal and Lacy exchanged. Chet was outspoken. "That's sure neat, old man. Wish I could shoot like that."

"Maybe you could, if you'd practice as much as I have," Jeff retorted.

"No, I'll have to go right now. I'd like to stay up here

another day, but I have to start in Monday down there, so
I haven't got any too much time," Chet said, firmly.

He shook hands with Lacy and Tom Neal, standing on
the bare, hoof-marked ground in front of the station.

"Well, here's luck. Come up again," they invited.

"Thanks. Will if I can. If you fellows ever get down
around Cottonwood, look me up."

He mounted his rangy, bright bay horse, and swung to
face the Julesburg trail. He held the horse in, while Jeff
walked alongside, holding to a tapadera, till they were out
of earshot of the two who stood at the station watching.
Then Chet reined up. "What is it, Jeff?"

Jeff fumbled in his trousers pocket. "Here," he said,
holding up a little stack of yellow coins, "you take this.
You're liable to need it. I got plenty."

"No, I don't want it. I can get along till I begin drawing
pay."

"I bet you do need it. You ought to get you a buckskin
suit. And a slicker. Have you got a slicker?"

Chet glanced down at his worn homespun. "I ain't got
much of a stake, but I don't like to be leaning on you."

"How about your doctor bill?"

"Mister Majors took care of that. . . . Well, if you say
so, I'll take twenty dollars, and get me some clothes, and pay
you back out of my first month's wages." He pocketed two
eagles, handing back the others Jeff would have pressed
upon him.

He held his right hand down, then, for a farewell clasp,
but Jeff was not quite through.

"Say, Chet—"

"What is it, Jeff?"

"I—I want you to be careful. Look out for holdups. Anderson and his bunch are still prowling around, and—"

"Don't worry about me. Lightning never strikes twice in the same place. You take care of yourself, best you can. I'll be all right."

He held out his hand again. Jeff clasped it hard. His one word of farewell was low and throaty.

In that moment, foresight touched Jeff uncannily. He saw the hawklike, menacing face of Pete Anderson. It seemed to leer between him and Chet. A chill ran through him, his whole body felt cold, save his throbbing wound. He braced himself resolutely, shaking his head, winking hard. As his eyes cleared of tears, he saw only Chet, galloping down the trail in the clear light of the April morning. He stood watching till his brother went out of sight behind a swell of the greening prairie, then turned and walked slowly back to the station.

The extra man made four round trips to Laramie with the mail. Jeff became more and more importunate. For the fifth trip they let him have his way about it, and go. He was, he said, as well as ever. Two scars, still livid, still shot with pain when he tensed his muscles, were not worth bothering about.

The trail to Fort Laramie seemed a great deal longer on his first trip—was a little longer. He swung out over the trackless green prairie instead of going through Lone Coulee. There was no need; no Indians were lurking there. He brought the eastbound mochila into Mud Springs on time, coming back, and the extra man, becoming talkative, spoke a word or two of cheer and farewell as he left with it for Julesburg.

Tom Neal did not wait to be asked for news, as he came in from Julesburg three days later.

"War's started!" he shouted, as he neared. He rode up gayly under the flooding light of the April morning, his eyes bright with excitement. "The Southerners took Fort Sumter! Bombarded it for two days! Lincoln has called for seventy-five thousand volunteers!"

Jeff glanced quickly at Lacy, standing beside him. "Where'd you hear that?" he demanded. "Sure about it?"

"You bet I'm sure! Kearny got it over the wire and the boys passed it along with the mail. I reckon there's a lot of dispatches in here about it, too." He swung the mochila over to Jeff.

"Did they kill a good many of 'em, when they took the fort?" Lacy asked.

"Unh-uh. Didn't kill a man on either side. That sounds kind of fishy, but Bill Kane says that's the straight of it— he brung the mail into Julesburg. Said the soldiers in the fort run out of grub, and knew there wasn't a chance in the world—they was surrounded ten to one—so they hauled down the flag."

Jeff clapped the mochila onto his waiting pony. He strapped his slicker; he rose to the saddle. In the instant of rising, he glimpsed a spot of color inside the cabin. Something bright moved there as the prairie breeze swept through the doorway. Red stripes and white, a star-spangled blue canton. The flag! It gave the dreary little station new meaning. A thrill ran through him. His upflung hand, as his pony hit its stride, was half a farewell to Neal and Lacy, half a salute to the floating emblem.

He told the news about Fort Sumter and the President's call for troops at relay stations and at Fort Laramie. "That's all I know about it, just what the rider from Julesburg told me," he replied again and again to soldiers and civilians who pressed for more news during his two-day wait at Laramie station for the eastbound mochila.

The mail got in early in the morning, and he headed east with it. He always had a feeling that the eastbound mail was not quite so important, so urgent, as that going west, though he handled one as carefully as the other. He was glad to know that now, East and West, he and Chet were partners, handling the selfsame mochila. The thought gave new meaning to the battered square of leather.

An uneventful, lonely ride brought Jeff into Mud Springs near nightfall. Tom Neal was ready; he swung the mochila down on his saddle with a resounding plop and moved off into the soft April dusk.

"Don't forget that paper!" Lacy yelled after him.

"Nope," came his reply, above receding hoofbeats.

"I told him to get a fresh newspaper and bring it up next time, if he had to pay a dollar for it," Lacy explained.

"Yeah, I'd like mighty well to see one, myself."

Lacy led Jeff's pony away to the stable. Jeff paced a turn or two on the trampled ground in front of the cabin, easing saddle-tired muscles, gratefully aware that his arrow wound was well, and that he felt as well as ever. Then he stepped in and lighted the lantern.

As its dull yellow light flared, he glanced above him. The flag was not there. He looked again; his eyes searched the dusky room. He moved around restlessly in the narrow space till Lacy showed in the doorway.

"What did you do with that flag?" Jeff demanded.

"Took it down."

"What for?"

"Got tired of seeing it up there."

"Where is it?"

"Don't get excited, now." Lacy's tone was deliberately provoking. He walked into the cabin. Jeff came to meet him.

"Hauling down the flag may go at Fort Sumter, but not out here," Jeff said, hardily. "Where'd you put it?"

"Where it won't bother anymore," Lacy taunted. Anger flared between them. The passion that was sweeping the continent surged into the lonely room.

Jeff laid his hand on Lacy's arm. Lacy struck it aside. The next instant, like springs let go, the partners came together.

Lacy aimed a blow at Jeff's face; Jeff dodged it. They clinched, and swayed back and forth over the dirt floor. They upset a chair and stepped into it with a crashing of rungs. They smashed against the stove; the stovepipe creaked and pans rolled and clashed.

Lacy braced a leg behind Jeff and threw all his heavier weight upon him. Jeff held taut as a steel rod, then all at once gave way. He clutched his opponent, jerked, and twisted as they went down. They fell hard. Jeff was on top. He held Lacy with fierce grip. "Where'd you put it?" he gritted.

No answer. Jeff twisted Lacy's collar tight with rope-hard fingers. "Come on," he said, grimly.

Lacy wiggled, striving to break the iron grip. His eyes bulged. Jeff twisted harder.

"Ow! Awk!" Lacy gasped. Jeff's fingers loosened ever so little.

"Over—in th' corner," Lacy panted.

Jeff let go and sprang to his feet. He gave Lacy, getting up slowly, an appraising look, then crossed to the corner where the other's glance had strayed. He tossed aside an old slicker, a blanket, a coil of rope, and brought up the flag.

He looked up, first, at the low roof-poles where it had hung before. Then, after a moment's thought, he strode to his bunk. He reached up and tied the tiny halyard tight to the rough-barked corner post at the compartment's head. "There!" he exclaimed.

Lacy walked out into the darkness without a word.

Jeff watched him go. His exultation began to fade. He was tired and hungry; he could feel the places where the arrow had hit him. He waited a little time, then when Lacy did not come back he made his supper of hardtack and cold beans.

The April night was mild; he left the door open, the lantern burning, and rolled into his bunk. Above him, its bright colors a blur in the dim light, he could see the flag. The sight warmed his lonely heart. He went to sleep.

A clatter and rattle at the stove roused him. He glanced over to see Lacy getting breakfast. The morning was foggy; the cabin stood in enshrouding mist, as lonely as a tiny craft upon a silent sea.

Something turned over in Jeff's heart at the sight of his partner. The flaring hate of last night seemed as far away as a dream. He crossed to the stove in two strides. "I'm sorry about—last night, Jack," he said, holding out his hand.

"So'm I," said Lacy. His hand met Jeff's. "Let's forget it."

"You bet."

The high-riding spring sun was warming the log-walled station when Tom Neal pulled up his lathered pony. He grinned impartially at Jeff and Lacy.

"Couldn't get a paper for you, for love nor money," he said, lightly. "Papers are scarcer than hen's teeth in Julesburg. Heard some news down there, though."

"What about?"

"Going to be a shake-up on the Express."

"How you mean?"

"They say the government has give the Butterfield outfit a contract for all the mail through here. They're gonna move their stuff up here off the Texas route. Some of 'em think it'll put Russell, Majors, and Waddell out o' business."

Lacy listened closely. Jeff stood in his tracks, stopped in the act of swinging into the saddle. "Reckon they'll keep on running the Express, won't they?" he queried.

"I don't know anything about it for sure," Neal returned. "A fellow can't tell what to believe, these days."

"One thing sure, the government never did anything for the Pony Express, nor for anybody that works on it," Lacy declared, caustically.

Jeff stood there like a figure in bronze, an American boy of that day, keen, hardy, self-reliant, unafraid. Soberly he spoke: "I don't want the government to do anything for me. I can do for myself."

He swung lightly into the saddle. The pair left at the station waved reply to his upflung hand as he rode away.

The fourth day after that Slade rode into Mud Springs, coming up the Julesburg trail. Jeff, back from Laramie only half an hour, stood beside Lacy and watched his coming. Without knowing it, they straightened, stood rigid, as he reined up his horse on the trodden space in front of the station.

"Good morning, Captain," they responded, to his word of greeting.

Jeff this time felt he was seeing the horseman's face with new, strange clearness. Pale, flinty, hard-lined, indomitable. The eyes, cold as blued steel, were the eyes of a man who had seen all things, and had tasted every experience save death.

Slade spoke pleasantly: "What do you need in the way of supplies?"

Lacy answered quickly, like one set free from tension. "We'll have to have a little wood before long, Captain. The oats is about all gone, and I reckon we ought to have some more bacon and hardtack."

Slade pulled out a memorandum book, penciled his notes. "Any signs of horse thieves?"

"No, sir, everything's been quiet."

"That's more than some stationmen can say." Slade's eyes darkened with a gust of passion. His voice carried sudden menace. "The second station east of Julesburg had every horse stolen the other night. There's one gang out here that's still causing a lot of trouble. If it's the last thing I ever do, I'm going to clean them up!"

In the silence, the swoop of the prairie wind sounded loud round the barren little station. Neither Jeff nor Lacy ventured to speak.

Then Slade's manner changed again. His eyes, now blue, twinkled with something very like good humor.

"How's that little bay acting, that I sent up here?" he demanded.

"He's a right good horse, sir," Jeff answered. "Does first rate."

There was a pause. Slade's eyes swung ahead; he seemed ready to touch spur to his horse. Lacy put the question Jeff had been wanting to ask: "Is there anything to this talk about the Pony Express stopping, Captain?"

"You needn't worry about that for a while yet, at least. Some changes are being made, though. The government has given the Butterfield line a mail contract on this route, effective July first. Russell, Majors, and Waddell are arranging to retain the management of the Express from St. Joe to Salt Lake City. The other outfit will run it from there on to California. The new mail bill Congress passed provides that the Pony Express is to keep on running during the continuance of the mail contract, or until an overland telegraph line is completed."

Slade shifted impatiently in his saddle. His eyes again sought the Laramie trail, a dark line across greening prairie slopes.

"Thank you, Captain," Lacy said.

"All right. Good day." He swung his horse around, and galloped away.

"Reckon the old Pony'll keep a-going, then," Jeff remarked, his eyes on the receding horseman.

"Yeah, you needn't worry about its stopping," Lacy agreed.

"Still, from what he said, looks like they might stop it if they build the telegraph line clean through."

"We'll be older and wiser than we are now before that happens," Lacy replied, sententiously. "Bet you the Indians would chop the poles down faster than they could set 'em up. . . . Confound it, I wish Tom had brought a paper."

The next time Tom Neal rode in from Julesburg he pulled a wadded newspaper from his pocket and hurled it at Lacy's head. "Take that!" he called, gayly. "Got it off'n a stage passenger by talking polite to him—and paying him four bits."

Lacy caught the paper neatly. "Wouldn't care if it cost a dollar—a fellow wants to know a little about what's going on these days." He unfolded the creased, brittle pages. Jeff, glancing back as his pony hit its stride, saw him walking slowly into the station, reading as he went, while Neal lounged outside with his tired pony.

Everything seemed the same to Jeff when he got back to Mud Springs, three days later. There was the usual hasty chaffing with Neal, a quick shift of the mochila to the other saddle. But the hoofbeats of Neal's pony had hardly died away when Lacy said, in queer-sounding voice: "Jeff, I sent in my resignation by Tom. I'm going home."

"Going home! What's the matter, Jack?"

"War! My state, Virginia, is in it! She's joined the Southern Confederacy! Ten thousand United States troops invaded Alexandria! The state authorities have twelve thousand soldiers at Richmond, and more coming! Troops from Carolina are coming up to help. The paper says they're marching into Gordonsville. That's right by my home. I'm going back!"

Jeff was watching his partner's face, bronzed again with the sun and wind of spring, his brown eyes lit with ardor. It was, he knew, no use talking. "What's the rush? Can't you stay on a while, and then go?"

"Not on your life! I want my share of the fun, and the fighting, too, if there is any. If I don't hurry it'll all be over before I get there, like as not. The paper says they're raising a troop of Virginia cavalry—that's what I want to get into. I'd have pulled out sooner, after I read about it, only I didn't want to leave you in the lurch."

"You don't need to stop on my account, if you think you ought to go. I'll get along somehow."

On a day a little later, the new stationman rode in from Julesburg. Lacy showed him the layout at cabin and stable. Then Lacy made up his blanket roll. He had picked out a seldom-used pony that needed to go down to Julesburg to be reshod, a saddle that needed repairs. His store of gold coin, his saved-up wages had been taken from their hiding place in the cabin and stowed away in a money belt. He was ready.

"You better chuck this job, too, Jeff," he suggested, as he tied his blanket roll. "Haven't you got enough of it yet?"

"I reckon I better stick," said Jeff, charily. He had no word for what was in his heart, his steadfast feeling for the whole Pony Express outfit, his warming thought that now every mochila he took from Mud Springs to Laramie had been across Chet's saddle before it came to him, that every mochila he brought down from Laramie would be handled by Chet further down the line. "How you going to go after you hit Julesburg?"

"I reckon they'll stake me to a pass on the stage—I'll go right through to St. Joe. Maybe stop off a day there—I've heard a lot about that Patee House being such a swell place, I'd like to stay there overnight and eat a couple of their meals. Then I'm going on to Virginia as fast as the trains will take me."

His pony's restless feet were crunching the gravel as he spoke. He held out a hard brown hand. "So long, Jeff, and good luck!"

Jeff, in an unsettling way, knew now that he had never known Lacy until this time. He had not liked Lacy's small fault-finding, his seeming lack of loyalty to anything. He saw him now, touched by his lot, his real self awake, starting across a continent to seek the face of danger. Saw, understood, and could say nothing. He winked fast; he forced a grin. His handclasp was strong. "Good-by! Take care of yourself!"

From a little way off in the clear, hard sunlight the new man, bearded, aloof, looked on indifferently.

"Well—" said Lacy.

Lightly he swung into the saddle. He flung up a hand in farewell; he rode away down the Julesburg trail. Jeff stood watching. Small and smaller the withdrawing figure under the flooding sunlight.

A dip in the trail hid him a while. He showed again at the top of the mile-away rise to the south. He halted there, sharp outlined against a steely sky. He swung his hat in a high circle, once, twice, three times. Then he spurred his pony down the further slope.

He was gone!

XIV   JEFF MEETS PETE ANDERSON

In August of 1861 the blue sky, remote and hard, the sun-dried buffalo grass, the hot sweep of the unresting winds were the same at Mud Springs as they had been a year before. The Pony Express, too, seemed the same, but change was on the way for it.

Jeff, slim, leather-hard, ready, stood in the blasting sunlight in front of the log-walled station. With keen gray eyes half shut against the searing wind, he watched the rider coming in from the south.

"That don't look like Tom," he remarked, while the horseman was yet several hundred yards away.

The bearded stationman narrowed his gaze. "Nope, it ain't," he agreed, carelessly.

The rider came up. His boyish face was burned brick-red;

his hair, under his old felt hat, showed yellow as wheat straw.

"Hello!" Jeff greeted. "Riding for Tom, this time?"

"Tom he quit."

"How'd that come?"

"He say he got tired this yob. Say purty soon wire be all up, Pony Express quit."

"Well, I don't know about that. I reckon it'll take 'em a long time yet. How far out are they now?"

"Got to Cottonwood yesterday, by yiminey!"

"Is that right! That's a hundred miles this side o' Kearny. And they're nearly two hundred miles east o' Fort Churchill, they say, coming out from the west end. I don't know—"

Jeff mounted, rode away.

The trail over which he rode to Laramie now showed the prints of many sharp-shod hoofs, the sun-baked ground bore fresh wheel tracks. The stage now ran daily. Jeff overtook the westbound coach near Chimney Rock, chucking along in ruts made years before by emigrant wagons. He waved and shouted to the lone driver, swung around the lumbering outfit, and galloped on. Its schedule was twenty days from the Missouri River to Placerville, California; the newspapers it carried were out-of-date by the time they got through, the letters stale. The Pacific coast still depended on the Pony Express as its carrier of urgent business letters, press dispatches covering the war, commercial news, and all military messages.

A few weeks before, the newspapers from Chicago and New York, wadded in the mail sacks in the boot of the dusty, swaying stage, had at the top of the editorial pages a clarion call:

"THE NATION'S WAR-CRY

"Forward to Richmond! Forward to Richmond! The Rebel Congress must not be allowed to meet there on the 20th of July. By that date the place must be held by the National Army!"

Then came the rout of the National Army at Bull Run.

News of the disaster was taken through the sagebrush country, to lone stations in the desert and on to the Pacific coast by the boyish couriers of the Pony Express.

The heart of the nation faltered. Then, youthful, sound, it rallied quickly. The stage Jeff overtook and passed was carrying newspapers of changed tone, sober, courageous:

"The Bull Run rebuff has stirred the North to a realizing sense of the dangers of the situation. The Government will now call to its aid the skill, the vigor, the integrity and the muscle of the country. We all appear to have overlooked the fact that the rebellion is guided and fanned by young, daring and vigorous men, who have staked their all on the struggle. . . . We must equal them in vigor and surpass them in preparation."

"Well, how goes it?" The tall, black-bearded young lieutenant had a way about him. Jeff turned gladly to face him in front of the sutler's store at Fort Laramie.

"All right, sir."

"Does carrying the mail get to be a tiresome grind?"

"I don't mind it. Once in a while, though, a fellow wonders whether it really amounts to much."

The lieutenant glanced keenly at Jeff. "Almost anyone

176

JEFF MEETS PETE ANDERSON

is likely to feel that way about his work sometimes," he said.
"But you may be sure that the Pony Express counts. Nothing in all the West outranks it just now in military and
political importance."

"Is that right?" Jeff asked, eagerly. He drew closer.
Steadfast as he was, a let-down mood was on him. He was
longing to have somebody tell him that his work was count-
ing for something.

"It is. Look here."

The lieutenant took an envelope and pencil from his
pocket, and sketched an outline map of the United States. He
blocked off with swift pencil strokes the western third of the
country's area—Texas and everything west of the main
range of the Rocky Mountains.

"There's a million square miles we've taken over in the
last fifteen years," he said, pointing to the blocked-off por-
tion of the map. "That is an empire in itself—more territory
than most nations have altogether. The ties that hold the
West to the older part of the country are still weak. Texas
seceded a few months ago, but we're going to do our best
to get her back again. But the same forces that took Texas
out of the Union are trying to get the upper hand in California. That would give them control of our whole Pacific
coast, and probably of the Mexican state Sonora. Then
the United States would be shut off from the Pacific,
and the whole future history of the continent would be
changed.

"What is holding California in line? General Edwin
Sumner, commanding the Military Department of the
Pacific, his troops, and the loyal people of the state. And

177

all of them are keeping in touch with the East through the Pony Express. They would be lost without it. Every trip you make these days, either way, you are carrying important dispatches between the government at Washington and General Sumner, Governor Downey, and the other leaders who are trying to save California for the Union. *Don't let anybody or anything interfere with that mail!*"

Jeff thrilled. Straight though he always stood, he now stood straighter. Hardship, loneliness, danger—what matter?

"I'm glad if it's worth while," he said, simply. "But if they get the wire through they probably won't need us anymore."

"I think the wire will go through. But that will not take away any of the credit due the Pony Express. California might have been lost to us before this, if it had not been for you boys. And nobody started to build a telegraph line through two thousand miles of wild country until the Express led the way. . . . I'll have to be going."

Jeff stood where he was. Again he resolved to stick to his task as long as there was a mochila to be carried, glad, that he and Chet, though separated, were both serving the Union cause.

Stub Olson, regular rider west out of Julesburg since Tom Neal quit, rode into Mud Springs in the lowering light of a late September afternoon. Jeff, standing beside a fresh and prancing horse, looked closely at him as he came up. "What's the matter, Stub?" he challenged. "Where's that grin of yours?"

The boyish Swede shook his head gloomily. "You hear about that faller gone by Cottonwood?" He stripped the mochila from his saddle and held it out to Jeff.

"What faller?" Jeff mimicked, settling the square of leather over his own saddle, while the stationman held the fretting horse.

"Express faller, bane gone now two days, think mabbe he bane killed—"

"What's his name?"

"Harr-low. He—"

Jeff had the Swede by the shoulders. "Tell me all about it! If anything's happened to Chet, I—I'll—"

That was all, Olson insisted. A riderless Express horse had come into Cottonwood station two days ago with the eastbound mochila on its saddle. Search showed no trace of the missing rider, Harlowe.

Jeff's right hand went unbidden to his holster. He faced the stationman. "Say, Al," he urged, "I better see about this. Can't you take the mail to Laramie, this once?"

"You know what my orders is. I'd just as lief ride up there as not, but I sure won't start out without an okay from Slade."

Jeff turned to the Swede. "How about you, Stub?" he pleaded. "Would you mind going on through with the mail, this time, so's I can get down to Cottonwood? That's Chet, my brother, that's gone!"

The Swede shook his yellow head. "Nope," he said, conclusively, "my orders bane go yust to Mud Springs, then wait for east mail."

Jeff wavered a moment, scanning stationman and rider.

179

Then his lips tightened, his face hardened. He jammed his old hat down, and swung into the saddle. His released pony's hoofs clattered on the sun-baked ground as he rode off on the Laramie trail without a backward glance.

The fourth day thereafter, about midforenoon, Jeff got back to Mud Springs with the eastbound mochila. When still half a mile out he noted a black horse tied to the cabin. As he got closer he saw it was one which Slade sometimes rode. As he pulled up his lathered pony in front of the station the well-set, hard-faced superintendent himself came out through the open doorway, followed by Olson. The stationman was hurrying up from the stable with a fresh mount.

Jeff swung down, tossed the mochila to Olson, and faced Slade. "Any news about my brother, sir?" he asked, eagerly.

"No. He's gone, that's all we know about him."

"Let me go and see if I can find him, Captain, won't you?"

"I don't think that would do any good, Harlowe." Slade's voice was not unkind. "We've had men out looking for him. The thing is to catch whoever waylaid him."

"Who do you think it was, sir?"

"Pete Anderson or some of his outfit. The Express and the stage won't be safe while he's alive. And the Express has to keep running now, they're depending on it out on the coast. . . . Get going, there," Slade ordered, sharply, turning on the wide-eyed Swede, who stood listening.

Olson scrambled into his saddle and spurred his pony down the Julesburg trail.

"Let me go with you, Captain, if you're out after Anderson," Jeff urged.

"I don't want to get you into a tight place. Anderson is quick on the draw, from all accounts."

"I'm not afraid of him!" Jeff blazed. "Let me go along!"

Slade's thin lips formed a wintry smile; he measured Jeff with a glance of cold, blue-gray eyes. "All right," he decided. "Get a fresh horse!"

Jeff ran to the stable and looked along the stalls. There stood the sweat-marked bay he had just ridden in, a roan that he knew had poor bottom, and Star, the rangy black that had carried him out of the Indian ambush. He threw a saddle and bridle on Star and led him up to the cabin.

"Better bring a blanket and some hardtack," Slade directed.

Jeff dashed into the cabin, found his heavy Colt revolver and shoved it into the right-side holster of his gun belt, grabbed a handful of hardtack and a box of cartridges for the light Smith and Wesson which he had worn in his left holster all the way from Laramie, rolled them in a blanket, and strapped it and his slicker behind his saddle. "I'm ready, sir," he exclaimed.

Slade was already in the saddle. He swung his horse; his hard glance brought the bearded stationman to attention. "If Harlowe isn't back here when the next mail comes up from Julesburg, you take it on to Laramie, Wilson," he said.

"All right, Captain."

Slade chirruped to his horse and headed into the Laramie trail. Jeff followed close on Star. They rode northward in the track a mile or so, then left it and bore northeast across trackless prairie, where the brown, curly buffalo grass softened the beat of their horses' hoofs.

A flock of white cranes rose ahead of them and flew away, whooping loudly. Wild geese took flight from sandbars as the riders came to the North Platte, dwindling in its wide bed. They forded it and galloped on into a country that became rougher. Stunted pine trees dotted the hillsides. The Black Hills of Dakota showed far to northward, like a blue, low-lying cloud on the horizon.

Slade led the way into an arroyo which split the brown hills. He drew rein where the ravine forked.

"This may be only a wild-goose chase," he said, low-voiced. "These two draws swing quite a ways apart and then come out fairly close together on a sort of tableland three or four miles above here. There's a trapper's shack about half-way up this right-hand draw, and it may be Anderson is using it for a hangout. I'll ride up the right-hand draw. You take the other one—we can meet up on the flat in about an hour. Watch as you go!"

Jeff swung his horse into the left fork of the arroyo. It soon turned sharply to the left. Its grassy banks were dotted with scrubby pines too low, too sparse, to break his view. He rode on, scanning the ground ahead. A strong wind strummed overhead and whipped the ravine with whirling gusts.

A couple of miles up, where a thicket of plum trees clung to its slanting sides, the arroyo changed course sharply. Jeff, from habit, loosened his Smith and Wesson in its holster as he rode closer to the turn. The curly grass muffled Star's hoof-beats. The wind roared hard.

He swung round the sharp turn and came face to face with Pete Anderson.

182

The outlaw, on a dun-colored pony, was as surprised as Jeff, but his hand went swift as a striking snake to a gun in his holster.

Jeff's draw was faster. Long practice focused for him in that split second. The Colt that flashed up in Anderson's hand was a clear-cut target. His Smith and Wesson cracked as the Colt leveled. The outlaw's gun jerked out of his grasp and spun to the ground. His hawklike face twisted with rage and pain; he let out savage maledictions.

"Put 'em up!" Jeff called.

Anderson's hands went up.

Jeff, his gun level, swung Star close to the outlaw's horse. He reached over with his left hand and drew Anderson's other gun from its holster, stuck it under his own belt. "Turn around and ride ahead slow," he ordered. "Don't try any tricks."

Anderson cursed, but wheeled his horse and rode on cautiously.

"Where you takin' me to?" he demanded, after they had ridden a little way.

"To Slade."

Anderson seemed to wilt in his saddle. He twisted to look at Jeff. "Look here," he wheedled, "I ain't wanting to see *him*."

Jeff made no reply.

"Ain't your name Harlowe?" Anderson asked.

"Yes."

"Say, look here! Wasn't that your brother what was ridin' outa Cottonwood?"

"Yes. Do—do you know anything about him?"

183

"Do I! Say, pard, looky here! Let's get together on this! I'll tell yuh where to find your brother, ef yuh'll just lemme go on about my business!"

Jeff's voice trembled. "Is he—dead?"

"Unh-uh! Not yet! Me an' my pard took him to a safe place—I figured ef I got in a tight corner an Express rider 'ud come in handy for tradin'. Turn me loose, and I'll tell yuh where to find him. Ef yuh don't, it'll go hard with him. He's tied up tight and nobody to wait on him. My pard backtracked this morning for other parts."

The world stood still for Jeff. He kept his gun on the outlaw by instinct; he hardly noticed that both horses had stopped. His mind whirled. Chet alive, needing help! He must go to him! And yet—

The captive saw him waver. He talked faster.

"I'll tell yuh where he is, honest I will! Jes' turn me loose; I'll tell yuh an' be on my way, an' nobody the wiser!"

The Pony Express, true carrier for a troubled nation! The battered mochilas which had to go! This shifty killer, who would kill again if set free!

Jeff saw it clear. He got a grip on himself. The gun in his hand became steady, as though cast in bronze. His voice had a steely ring:

"Ride on!"

"Hold on! I'll tell yuh, right now, ef yuh'll lemme go!"

Jeff motioned significantly with his gun. "Go ahead, pronto!"

They rode single-file out of the arroyo and topped the bleak tableland. It stretched before them bare save for two dead pine trees whose jagged branches showed stark against the lowering sky. A man on a black horse rode toward them from where he had waited near the trees.

Slade's flint-like face showed a flicker of approval as he neared. "A good piece of work," he said. "Where did you get him?"

Jeff told.

"Keep him covered just a minute more." Slade swung down, took a strip of rawhide from his pocket, and tied the outlaw's hands behind him.

"I'll take care of him now," Slade said, with deadly finality. His quick glance touched the lariat at his saddle horn, the jagged limbs of the blasted pines. "Ride back the way you came, Harlowe. Wait for me half a mile down the draw. Go now." His level voice was as implacable, as cold as Fate.

Jeff's hands shook as he put his gun back in its holster. He wheeled his horse, forced him to a gallop. He rode, and did not look back.

XV   DOWN THE TRAIL

HE was heart-sick, and trembling from something more chilling than the cutting wind that whipped along the arroyo when Slade rode down to him. Slade rode alone. The lariat that had hung on his saddle was gone. Jeff watched him draw near, not daring to speak.

"Well, that fellow did one white thing at the last minute, anyhow," Slade said, briskly. "He owned up to kidnapping your brother, and told me where to find him. You can start up there the first thing in the morning."

Jeff, white-faced, staring, found his voice. "Hadn't I better start right now, sir?"

Slade glanced at the sky, on which evening was lowering.

186

"No, you couldn't make it in the dark. It's full twenty miles from here, in rough country. In the morning I'll tell you how to go, and let you have my compass. I'm going to hunt for Anderson's partner tomorrow. I turned his horse loose, it was no good. . . . Let's look around for some dry wood. I have a little slab of bacon, we'll broil it to go with our hardtack. Are you hungry?"

Jeff thought he could not eat, but when the hardtack and bacon was ready he did eat, squatting by the little fire, stealing glances at his companion. The flickering firelight touched Slade's face, lighting it as Jeff had seen a weathered butte light up when storm clouds broke apart overhead. The thin, straight lips looked fuller, the square face with its low cheek bones less implacable, in this softening glow. But Jeff, thinking of the missing lariat, remembering the dried ear, shivered.

More than for food, more than for rest after his long saddle grind, he longed for morning to come, so that he could go to save Chet. Wrought up with fear and longing, he lay awake in his blanket, glancing now at the stalwart, dimly outlined figure lying beside him, now at the dying fire, hearing the lessened wind soughing down the arroyo, the two horses munching along the picket line. At last he slept, thinking to wake very early. He woke when Slade shook him. It was day.

"Better get going," Slade said. "We won't stop for breakfast." He drew his memorandum book from his pocket, and tore a sheet from it. "Here, I've drawn a rough map for you. Take this along, and the compass. Go back up this draw to the flat, head northwest for this butte, and due north from it. You'll come to another butter, with a patch of pines on the south side. Look for a shack in the edge of the pines. . . ."

Jeff forced back the sagging, weather-beaten door, saw the prone figure in the gloom, spoke huskily: "Chet, is that you?"

"Sure is. Got a knife? This rawhide is mighty tight."

Jeff slashed the lashings on Chet's wrists, on his ankles, helped him sit up. "Are you all right?" he demanded.

"I reckon so, if I just had a drink."

Jeff glanced around the bare, tiny shack, looking vainly for any sort of vessel. Then he hurried out, crossed to the trickling spring he had noticed on the hillside, and came back with half a hatful of water.

"M-m!" Chet drank deep. "That sure tastes good!"

"Well, how in the world did they get the best of you?"

"Two fellows rode up alongside of me, one grabbed my pony's bit and the other one cracked me over the head with his gun. That's the last I knew, till I was on the way up here, tied on a horse. 'Twas Anderson and another chap. I didn't have time to draw when they tackled me." Chet rubbed his head.

"Anderson won't bother anymore. I'll tell you about it after while. Can you ride now, d'you think?"

"Sure, I can."

"Then let's go. It's quite a ways down there, and we'll have to ride double and go slow. . . . We ought to get back as soon as we can. The way they're stringing that wire, I reckon the Express won't be making many more trips. We've stayed with it this far—we sure want to be on the wind-up."

"Then this will be the last trip, will it, sir?"

Slade seemed not to hear. Straight, well-poised, he stood outside the open doorway of the Mud Springs station, the bridle rein of his black horse in his hand. The gloomy light of the October afternoon was on his face.

Jeff watched him in the silence. As he watched, the dull clouds parted; the slanting sunlight lit the bare little cabin, the hoof-marked ground where they stood. Slade's reddish-brown hair glinted in the sun. His blue-gray eyes swung on Jeff.

"What was it you said?"

Jeff repeated his question.

"Yes, this mail that is now on the way will be the last one for the Pony Express. The telegraph line is clear through." His glance, like Jeff's, turned to the single strand of iron wire, strung on green cottonwood poles, that passed within a few yards of the station. "You can get your final pay at Julesburg."

"All right, sir. What about the horses? What are they going to do with them?"

"Use some of the best ones on the stage line, sell some. The stationmen will look after that."

The bare, hard cabin gloomed again as clouds hid the sun.

"There's a horse here I'd like to have, Captain. That black—Star's his name. He's the one I rode that day the Indians chased me, and that time when I went up and got Chet. I like him, somehow."

189

"All right, if you care to buy him."

"What'll you take for him?"

"Well, you've been the most dependable rider on the division. If you want that black horse, take him along for seventy-five dollars. And pick out a good saddle, I'll throw that in. . . . Where are you going to go, Harlowe?"

The unresting wind of the high plains soughed around the cabin. The wire strummed on the cottonwood poles.

"Chet is coming on up here after he makes his last ride with the mail. Then as soon as I get back from my trip to Laramie we'll pull out together. We're going to ride down to Denver, and go East from there."

"Fine! Well, I'll be on my way. Have to get back to Julesburg." Slade gathered his reins. "Is that price all right for the black?"

"Yes, sir, it sure is—he's worth a good deal more than that. I'm ever so much obliged to you. Shall I settle for him out of my final pay, or—"

"That will be all right, of course. I'll tell the Julesburg agent. He'll attend to it if I'm not there when you come through. Good-by, in case I don't see you again, and good luck."

Slade held out a muscular, well-shaped hand. Jeff grasped it. In that instant he seemed to stand outside himself. Prevision touched him. He heard himself say: "Good-by, Captain, and good luck to you!"

He was looking squarely into Slade's broad-cheeked, grim, thin-lipped face, lined with hard living. He knew, strangely, there was no good fortune for this man. A cold thrill touched him uncannily. The black fate that waited for Slade cast its chill around them both.[18]

190

Fleeting as the grip of a hand, this feeling. Then Jeff stood watching Slade ride out of sight down the trail, while evening darkened upon the high plains and the wind strummed over the wire.

Jeff rode into Laramie station, swung off his horse, and in the same easy motion stripped the battered brown mochila from his saddle and passed it to the waiting rider.

"Here you are, Joe," he said, with a grin. "Last time I'll bother you." [14]

The hard, slim lad laughed as he caught the square of leather. "It ain't our fault, anyhow, is it?" he queried. "We stayed right with it."

"We sure did. What're you going to do now?"

"Think I'll head for the coast. How about you? Going to go to war?"

Jeff's face sobered. His gray eyes, keen, unafraid, looked straight ahead. "I expect we'll both be in it, my brother and I."

"Well, here's luck, old man!"

And Joe was away, heading for the high foothills and the mountain passes.

"Come on, Jeff, let's go!"

Chet, with easy grace, swung his bright bay horse around as it pranced and reared over the hard-trodden ground in front of the Mud Springs station. He was as eager as his horse to be away.

Jeff, in the doorway, deliberately hitched his gun belt. He stood slim and stanch in worn buckskin, his face leather-brown under his old felt hat. A money belt, lined with gold coin, the saved wages he had dug up from his cache, bulged his clothes at the waist. "I reckon I'm ready," he said.

Then he took a last look into the cabin. The sweep of his steady gray eyes went round the hard little room, become half homelike to him. Now he was going. Leaving this place was saying good-by to the Pony Express.

In that quick moment he thought of Lacy, of Bill Johnson, of Tom Neal. And Alex Carlyle! Gone, all.

But Chet was here! Jeff's heart warmed; a thrill ran through him.

He faced outside. Star, the rangy black horse he liked, his own now, stood there ready. The saddle, even with a blanket roll at the cantle, looked strange and bare. The mochila was gone.

The sunlight was clear and hard, the sharply slanting sunlight of late autumn on the high northern plains. The short grass rippled coldly in the wind.

Jeff swung into the saddle, brought the black around beside Chet's bay. They rode away together down the empty sun-browned trail.

The wind, the cadence of hoofbeats, went with them; strong the wind, the hoofbeats fleet.

NOTES

[1] Page 55. J. A. Slade served as a private in Company A, First Illinois Infantry, from May 4, 1847, till honorably discharged October 16, 1848. He enlisted at the age of eighteen. This regiment went through the Mexican War.

[2] Page 55. The description of Slade's height, build, complexion, and general appearance, and the matter of his eyes changing color comes from Mr. Lew L. Callaway, an attorney of Helena, Montana. Mr. Callaway as a youth lived in the family of Captain James Williams, who once arrested Slade. Callaway knew Amede Bessette, a Frenchman who worked for the Overland Stage under Slade, and has talked with others who personally knew the famous frontiersman.

[3] Page 75. This story of Slade comes from Mr. Burton Carey, Virginia City, Montana. It was related to him by the late George E. Gohn of Virginia City, whose father was in the first Montana gold rush. Mr. Carey's grandfather was well acquainted with Slade.

[4] Page 84. This Smith & Wesson seven-shot revolver was invented about two years before the time of the story. It was the model largely used by Northern officers in the Civil War.

[5] Page 88. Dispatch in the *New York Tribune*, November 8, 1860.

[6] Page 91. *Ibid.*, November 9, 1860.

[7] Page 91. *Ibid.*

[8] Page 91. *Ibid.*

[9] Page 93. The time as given here is based on press dispatches in the *New York Tribune* and the *San Francisco Bulletin* of November, 1860, and is believed to be correct.

[10] Page 105. *Ibid.*

[11] Page 108. The only printed account of this tragedy I have

195

ever found is a brief dispatch from Fort Kearny appearing in the *New York Tribune* of December 27, 1860.

[12] Page 141. *New York Tribune*, March 4, 1861.

[13] Page 190. After the Pony Express stopped, Slade retained for a time his position as Superintendent of the Julesburg Division of the Overland Stage. But his sprees were becoming harder and more frequent, and when he wrecked the sutler's store at Fort Halleck the stage company let him out. He drifted to the Montana gold fields in the spring of 1863, and soon was feared by the most hardened men there. After one of his shooting scrapes the Vigilantes issued a warrant for his arrest. He tore it up and defied them. For this they hanged him, March 10, 1864. His body lies in the Mormon graveyard at Salt Lake City, Utah.

[14] Page 191. The transcontinental telegraph line was completed October 24, 1861. The Pony Express stopped running the last week in October, 1861.

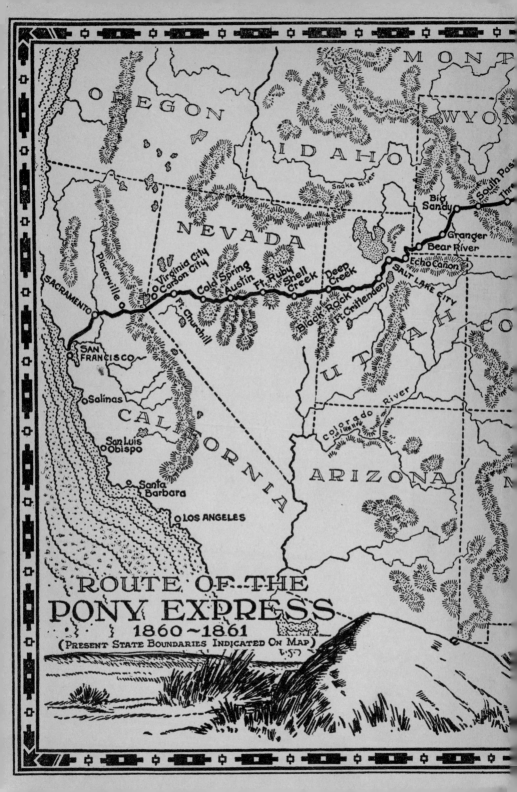

ROUTE OF THE
PONY EXPRESS
1860 ~ 1861
(PRESENT STATE BOUNDARIES INDICATED ON MAP)